DOGNAPPED!

Randy's cocker spaniel, Joe, is lost. But what gets the Digital Detectives really worried is that a pattern of dog disappearances is emerging all over Crescent Bay. Is Joe just another victim of this rash of dognappings? And who is behind them? Is it just a matter of rivalry between dog breeders for the upcoming county show or is it part of a plot to conduct genetic research on canines?

To solve the mystery, you'll make on-line investigations of the headquarters of a mysterious web site claiming to be run by dogs, the Highlands Kennel Club dog show, and a place called Dogwood. Analyze every fingerprint, interrogate every suspect, and record everything in your on-line crime journal. Remember: If you miss a single clue, you might not live to solve another case.

For Joe

enhance
NOW

9   8   7   6   5   4   3   2   1
Digit on the right indicates the number of this printing

Library of Congress Cataloging-in-Publication Number 00-134990

ISBN 0-7624-0962-2

Digital Detectives Mysteries® developed by enhanceNOW,
Carla Jablonski, and Jay Leibold

Designed by Bill Jones and Jan Greenberg
Cover illustrations © 2001 by Mike Harper
Series Editor: Carla Jablonski
Running Press Editor: Susan K. Hom
Typography: Minion, Futura, Letter Gothic, and Orbital

This book may be ordered by mail from the publisher.
Please include $2.50 for postage and handling.
But try your bookstore first!

Running Press Book Publishers
125 South Twenty-second Street
Philadelphia, Pennsylvania 19103-4399

Visit us on the web!
www.runningpress.com

THE SCENT
OF
CRIME

by Jay Montavon

RUNNING PRESS
Philadelphia • London

CHAPTERS

WELCOME, DIGITAL DETECTIVE!

The first time you log on to the Digital Detectives web site,

http://www.ddmysteries.com

you will be required to choose a user name. Once you have received your user name, write it in the space below.

_____

Digital Detective User Name

Your user name will bookmark your investigative work on the web site, so that you can continue where you left off.

WARNING:

This is *not* a typical mystery. You *should not* read every page of this book—that would spoil many of the story's best surprises! You will be directed on-line at certain points to gather evidence from the crime scenes. The web site will tell you which page of this book to return to. Do a good job, and you'll solve the crime! Make a sloppy investigation and . . . well, some *very* bad things can happen . . . .

Good luck!

1
THE MISTAKE

You and your friends Tina Garrett and Jack Hertz stomp your feet on the wooden bleachers. Left, right, left, right. The three of you chant with each stomp. "Let's go, Ran-dy! Let's go, Ran-dy!"

You're at a match between your friend Randy Rivers' soccer club and their crosstown rivals. The other people in the stands glance over at you, then hunch down under their coats. A drizzle swirls out of the gray sky. During a pause in the action, Randy looks up at you from the soccer field and draws his finger across his throat. He wants you to shut up.

You look at Jack who looks at Tina, who shrugs. She lifts her right foot again and stomps it down on a weather-washed plank. "Let's go, Ran-dy! Let's go, Ran-dy!"

Randy's black cocker spaniel, Joe, is seated next to you. He winces with each stomp and shout. "Hey, guys, we should cool it," you tell Tina and Jack. "We're getting on Joe's nerves."

"Oh, if we're bothering Joe . . ." Tina says. She and Jack settle down. Randy rolls his eyes at you with exasperated relief.

Tina cups her hands around her mouth. "We're not cheering for you Randy," she yells. "We're just trying to keep warm!"

Tina is the most rambunctious of the crew. Jack, a.k.a. Satellite Jack, is unique in his own way, which mostly has to

1

do with being a genius and inventor of high-tech gear. Randy is fourteen, a year older than the rest of you, and a natural leader. You're the newcomer in the group; you moved here last summer from Colorado. Together the four of you are called the Digital Detectives.

The Digital Detectives are the best thing that could have happened to you. You weren't sure at first about Crescent Bay, a small fishing and farming city on the California coast, which has been changing lately due to an influx of high-tech business. The old Crescent Bay people and the new ones don't always get along. Not only did you find three great friends in Randy, Jack, and Tina, but you've made a name for yourself around town. In your first case you unmasked the maker of a killer computer game virus. Your second case solved the mystery of strange events in a creepy abandoned house atop an ocean bluff.

A whistle blows on the field, announcing the end of the first half. Twenty-two mud-streaked players, including Randy, trot to the sidelines. You stand up and stretch.

"Let's take a walk," you suggest to Tina and Jack.

"We need to move around and get warm," Jack agrees.

The match is still scoreless. There was a lot of amusing slipping and sliding in the first half, but no goals. The rain came down hard this morning. It turned the field into a bed of mud. The storm let up before game time, but a steady drizzle still falls. Sitting on hard wood benches while you get slowly soaked will not be in this week's highlight reel.

The three of you are here because of your loyalty to Randy, who's one of the most loyal people you've ever met. He offered to excuse you from your promise to attend when the rain was pouring this morning. But you couldn't let Randy down. It's his biggest game of the season. Plus, Joe comes to all his matches, and Randy's parents couldn't make it today. So you knew you needed to be here to look after the dog.

Joe gives an expectant look when Tina and Jack stand up too. "Sorry, boy," you tell the cocker spaniel. "There's another half of soccer to be played. We're just stretching our legs."

Still, Joe bounds down the bleacher steps. That's what you love about him. He does everything with such glee. His front legs leap down each step and his back legs scramble to keep up, his whole shaggy body wriggling. His tongue lolls happily and his eyes are bright.

Joe gazes up at you from the bottom of the bleachers, lip snaggled on a front tooth. Tina runs after him and mushes his little face between her palms. "Ooh, Joe, you are the cutest dog-faced boy in all of Crescent Bay!"

He laps at her nose and cheeks. Jack walks down more slowly, his hands stuffed in coat pockets, his shoulders hunched. He wrinkles his nose at all the licking, but you just smile. You have to agree with Tina. Joe does seem almost human. He seems to follow every word of your conversations. He cocks his head when you ask a hard question—not any question, only the hard ones. And he gets a crestfallen look on his face when he's not invited on an outing. You feel like he's just another member of the Digital Detectives.

You check for Randy as you walk across the soccer field, but he's in a meeting with his team. Then you remember the leash in your pocket. You'd better put it on Joe. He comes when you call, and you clip on the leash.

The park you're in is called Portola Grove. It's high in the hills, at the eastern edge of town. On a clear day you can see the city below. Beyond it stretches the Pacific Ocean. There's a playground in the park, and a soccer field, and a big grassy area where people throw frisbees and walk their dogs. Behind the open area is a deep wood that runs all the way up to the top of the coastal mountains above Crescent Bay.

With Joe straining at the leash, you join the other dog walkers in the open area near the wood. "Look at all these people—and dogs," you marvel. "On such a dismal day."

"The dogs don't mind," Tina notes. "More mud equals more fun."

Suddenly Joe sprints to join a cluster of dogs, ripping the leash out of your hand. The dogs are busy jumping up on each other and chasing around. Joe stops short and waits, his ears pricked.

A terrier and a German shepherd come to check him out. Joe shows no fear. His ears stay alert and his tail high. Even with the shepherd, Joe doesn't give ground. This causes the shepherd's tail to lower a bit. It's harder to tell what's happening with the terrier, because its tail is clipped very short.

"Is this dog with you?" a voice asks.

You look up. A young woman wearing a beret is talking to you. Frizzy amber hair sticks out from under the hat. Her face is narrow, with high cheekbones and twinkling green eyes.

"Sort of," you answer. "He belongs to our friend Randy."

"*Belongs?*" the woman says. "Maybe you mean that Randy is his caretaker."

"Yeah, that's right," Tina agrees. "I heard there was a movement to change the term 'pet owners' to 'caretakers.'"

This brings a grin from the woman. "Exactly! That was my idea. People who think they own dogs think they can do anything to them. Look at that poor terrier, with her tail cut

4

off. Can you imagine how it hurt? Plus she's got no way to express herself now. A tail is a dog's way of talking."

"Yeah, I never thought of that," Tina says. "Who's her, uh, caretaker?"

She nods toward a man in an overcoat, scarf, and cap. "Him."

He's watching the terrier. "Teresa, come here right now!" he commands.

"He's a breeder." The woman says it as if it's a dirty word.

The terrier puts what little she has of her tail between her legs and goes running to the man. Joe and the German shepherd have decided to be friends. They start putting their paws up on one another and nipping playfully.

"Joe's tail is clipped too," you muse. "But it's a little longer."

"That's better than nothing," the woman says, but adds sternly, "It's still a terrible thing for Randy to have done."

Joe has gotten tangled up in his leash while he's playing. Jack, who's been standing to one side looking a little bored, says, "I'll fix it."

When you turn back to Tina, she has found out that the woman's name is Molly. You introduce yourself and shake hands.

"So do you know all the dogs around here, Molly?" Tina asks.

"Sure. I'm up here at least twice a day. I'm with that spotted one over there. And the retriever with the broken leg. And the sort of thin one jumping right now. And the part-samoyed, too."

"Wow. So half of them are yours!" Tina exclaims.

"Well . . . I'm *with* them," Molly replies.

Jack comes back holding Joe's leash. You notice something

extra dangling from the leash. "Jack, you didn't have to take his collar off, too," you say.

"He wouldn't hold still," Jack complains. "I couldn't get the leash unhooked, so I just took off the whole thing."

While Tina and Molly keep talking, you and Jack watch the dogs play. Joe has joined another knot of dogs. He's sniffing around an even bigger one now, a rottweiler.

Suddenly a cheer sounds from the soccer crowd behind you. You wheel around to see Randy racing up the field, his arms high in the air. His teammates are grabbing his jersey. The other team's goalkeeper boots the ball away in disgust.

"Randy just scored a goal!" you cry.

"About time," Jack remarks.

"It's the first goal of the game," you go on. "And we missed it. He'll kill us if he finds out."

"Don't worry, we'll ask someone how he scored," Tina says.

"I guess you need to get back to the game," Molly says, raising a mittened hand to wave good-bye.

Tina waves back. "See you later."

"Come on, let's get Joe," you say.

You call his name again, several times. But he doesn't emerge from the group of dogs.

"Where'd he go?" Jack asks.

You walk a big circle around the dogs and owners. You're sure Joe's head will pop out at any moment. But it doesn't. And he doesn't come running when you keep calling his name.

What's worse, no one has seen him in the last few minutes. "Just a sec," Tina says. She runs to catch up to Molly, who is taking her dogs back to her car. But Tina comes back a minute later with her head hanging. Molly hasn't seen Joe either.

"This can't be happening," you moan.

"Let's keep looking," Tina says.

But fifteen minutes later, you've covered every bit of the park. You've even poked your head into the woods and called for Joe. He's nowhere to be seen.

"I can't believe it," Tina wails as you trudge back to the soccer field. "Joe's gone!"

"Now Randy's *really* going to kill us," you say miserably.

2
THE SEARCH

The moment you dread has come. The soccer match is over. Randy is the hero. His goal won the game. After he's done celebrating with his teammates, he joins you in the stands. You see the big grin on his face, his dark hair hanging in wet strands over his eyes, his brown eyes glowing. You don't know how you're going to tell him the news.

"So did you see my goal?" he asks.

There's an awkward moment before Jack says, "You streaked down the right side, got past two defenders, and then used the outside of your left foot to slice the shot in."

Randy does a double take. "Wow, Jack, I didn't realize you were getting into the game so much. Thanks, man."

"You're fantastic, Randy," Tina exclaims. "Totally amazing. Awesome, even."

This brings a funny look from Randy, because Tina doesn't usually gush like that. She's pretty tough on the outside—especially when she's roaring down the side-walk at you on her skateboard, her elbows, wrists, and knees wrapped in futuristic leather-metal protection pads, her eyes masked by dark blades, her sandstone-red hair streaming out from under her helmet. But then she stops, flips up her board, and smiles, showing her chipped front tooth. You know you're all really important to her, kind of like family. The only other family Tina has at home is her dad.

Randy cocks his head at Tina for a minute before he answers, "Yeah, thanks Tina."

Then he looks down. You can feel it coming. The pit of your stomach feels like it's crawling with caterpillars.

"Where's Joe?"

You step up. Randy left Joe in your care, so you're the one who has to give him the news. You take a deep breath. It feels like your chest is about to cave in. "We're not sure where Joe is. We took him for a walk over there with the other dogs, and then suddenly—he was gone."

A look of panic flashes through Randy's eyes. He struggles for a moment to get it under control. Then he stretches his arms behind his head. You can tell he's trying to act casual. "Well, Joe would never run away. I'm sure we'll find him," he says.

"We looked everywhere in the park," Tina tells him.

Randy narrows his eyes, thinking. "Hmm. We can look again. Even if we don't find him, I'm sure somebody else will. All the information is on his dog tags."

Jack holds out the leash. Attached to the leash is the collar, and attached to the collar are the dog tags. "I, uh, took these off, kind of by accident."

"What? Why'd you do that?" Randy cries, grabbing the leash.

Jack shrinks back, looks down, and takes a moment to remove his glasses, which are wet from the rain. The glasses are round. So is Jack's face and his plump pink cheeks. With his soft lips and fine brown lashes, he has a vulnerable look. Sometimes it fools people into thinking they can take advantage of him. Usually they're sorry they try, because they run into his razor-sharp mind. He has supreme confidence in his intellect. But right now that's gone, and his outward expression matches his inner state.

"I'm a complete moron," Jack mumbles.

Randy stares at the leash as if in a daze. Slowly he recovers himself. He puts a hand on Jack's shoulder and says, a bit half-heartedly, "Don't worry, we'll find him."

You're amazed that Randy can keep his emotions as under control as he is. If it was you, and Joe was your dog, you'd probably be screaming at your friends. But that's the way Randy is. He's the one telling you everything will be all right, instead of the other way around. Whenever you've been in a tight spot with him, Randy has always been able to make you feel like you'll come through.

Still, his eyes remain fixed on a waterlogged bleacher bench. He hasn't been able to look at any of you directly since you told him the news.

Tina hates these awkward moments. "Let's get to it, then. We'll scour the park one more time."

Jack fits his glasses back over his eyes with care, then consults his watch. "Yeah, my mom will be here to pick us up any minute. Let's go."

* * *

The ride home with Satellite Jack's mom, Judy, is glum. You only had a couple of minutes to look for Joe before she pulled up and honked in her beat-up old Volvo. You were pretty sure you weren't going to find him anyway, but Randy wanted to look for himself.

11

Now you sit squeezed next to Tina and Jack in the back seat. Randy's in front with Judy. She has a breezy manner to go along with her lively face and tight, dark curls. Like the rest of Jack's family, she tends to be preoccupied with her thoughts. She's a former computer scientist who now spends half her time painting and half her time promoting open access to the Web. Jack's dad is in computers, too. They made a ton of money in the first big tech rush in Silicon Valley, and then retired to Crescent Bay.

The scary thing is, Jack's probably smarter than both of them. At first you wondered how they felt about that. But since they provide him with all the components he needs to assemble his high-tech inventions, you figure they must be into it.

Judy guides the car down the hilly streets toward the flat part of town. This is where you, Tina, and Randy live. Randy's house is across the street from you, and Tina's is the next block over. Jack lives up in the hills, where the more expensive houses are.

"Can you take us to Randy's?" Tina asks. "We need to work on something there." Randy gives her a questioning look. "We'll make posters to put up for Joe," she adds.

"Joe?" Judy asks.

Randy clears his throat. "My dog. He got lost at the park."

"Oh yeah . . ." Judy replies. "We did take him up there with us, didn't we?"

She pulls into Randy's driveway, and you all pile out. Judy waits for Jack to slide into the front seat, but he says, "I need to be here too, Mom. It's kind of important. Can you pick me up later?"

She nods absently. "Maybe . . . well, call us. Have fun."

"Right, Mom."

Jack closes the car door and you troop into Randy's house. The first thing Randy does is check the phone message machine. But there's nothing about Joe.

The rest of you drop your coats in the front hall. Your clothes are damp and they stick to your skin. But you're glad Tina thought of the idea of making posters. At least you'll be doing something to redeem your mistake.

Randy leads you down the hall to his room. He flops down on the bed, his clothes still covered with mud. A brown streak runs down the side of his face. Tiny dirt clods hang in his hair.

Tina grabs a piece of paper and lies on the floor. "I'll design the poster."

You sit in front of Randy's computer. "Maybe there are some web sites for lost dogs. Is it all right if I go on-line?"

Randy nods silently. While you connect, Tina sketches two boxes and some lines of text. "We'll have pictures of Joe in the poster so everyone can see how good-looking he is. You can put this all together on the computer, right Jack?"

"Of course," Jack says. "Where are we going to get the photos?"

You raise an eyebrow at Jack and glance around the room. Jack follows your gaze. Joe is in half the pictures. Jack knocks his forehead. "Duh. Okay, I'll take a few of these pictures with me and scan them into the computer. Then I can output copies of the poster on my color printer."

"Great," Randy says to the ceiling.

Tina admires one of the pictures. Her voice rises an octave. "Ooh, don't worry, Joe, we're going to find you. You're the cutest boy with a dog face in the whole wide world!"

"Look at this," you announce, staring at Randy's computer screen. "It's a web site called TheDogBytes.com. 'For dogs only, by dogs only,' it says. All the messages are from dogs. Like this one."

Watch out for the new fence on Chestnut Street. I was out sniffing my usual route and ran smack into it. —Kiki42

"Cool," Tina says. "I'll write one for Joe. 'Help me, I got lost in Portola Grove. I wasn't paying attention and some dweeb took off my collar . . .'"

"I'm not a dweeb," Jack objects. "I'm a geek."

"I'll post the same message on this web site," you say to Tina.

All of a sudden Randy lifts his arm to look at his watch. "What time is it?" you wonder.

"Five-thirty," Randy muses. He groans and raises himself to a sitting position. His head hangs and he stares at the floor. "Every day at exactly this time, Joe sits down in front of me with this expectant look. He's saying, 'I'm ready for my biscuit.' It never fails. You could tell time by that dog."

There's a moment of silence, then Tina asks, "Do you get a cookie too?"

Finally Randy cracks a smile. "Yeah. I guess we all deserve a cookie right now."

* * *

The next morning, Jack is ready with the posters. You've agreed to rise early to put them up. You and Randy ride to Jack's house, since it's near Portola Grove. Jack has the posters neatly packaged in his briefcase. Randy puts the briefcase in his bike basket, and you set off.

You cover the blocks around the park with the notice about Joe, posting it on telephone poles, trees, anything you can find. Yesterday's rain has stopped, but the ground is still soaked. Misty wisps curl from the lawns and blooming gardens of the neighborhood.

Spring is a funny time in Crescent Bay. On the one hand, things start blooming early, especially the fruit trees. Fragrances of cherry and plum blossom waft through the air. But then a monster storm will come barreling in from the Gulf of Alaska, bringing cold winds and heavy rains that strip the trees of their petals. The one good thing about those big storms is that they also bring good swells for surfing.

As you move on to a new block, you notice an older man wearing a jacket and cap. He's coming toward you at a brisk clip, taking his dog for a walk. The man pauses to watch you. His dog, a dalmatian, sits neatly by his side.

"Lost a dog, eh?"

"Yes, he's a black spaniel," Randy replies. "His collar came off. Have you seen him?"

The man peers at the poster. "I'm sorry, but I haven't. He looks like a mighty good fella. I just hope Dooley hasn't gotten his hands on him."

"Dooley?" you ask.

The man's lips purse. "If you haven't met up with Dooley, then you're lucky. He's the dog control officer around here. Enjoys his job a little too much, I think."

"Of course," Randy realizes. "We should check the dog pound and see if Joe got picked up."

"Wouldn't surprise me," the man says. "Well, I hope you

find him."

"Thanks!" You wave to him, encouraged by the exchange. If everyone in the neighborhood is this helpful, then your chances of finding Joe are better.

But the next block is a different story. While Jack holds a poster for you to tack to a tree, you hear a house door slam behind you. It's followed by footsteps and a woman's angry voice.

"What do you think you're doing, you kids?"

You look up to find a woman with tangled orange-blond hair, tiny features, and narrow eyes shaking her fist at you. She's wearing a tattered old bathrobe and black shoes. You quickly remove the tacks and show her the poster.

"We're sorry, ma'am," you explain. "It's just that we lost our dog and—"

She grabs the poster from you. "Your dog? You're ruining my tree for some mangy dog?"

Randy approaches from the other side of the street. "Please don't give them a hard time. They're just helping me out."

The woman jerks her head up. "This shaggy 'Joe' thing belonged to you?" She reads the poster, then tears it into shreds. "Well, you can forget about it. You'll never see him again. Not if you lost him around here."

With that she turns, clip clops back up the walk, and slams her front door. The three of you stare after her, dumbfounded. Only when you notice the man with the dalmatian walking back up the block do you return to your senses.

He gives you a sympathetic smile as he passes. "I see you've met Elly Shotte."

"Yeah, I guess we did," Randy says.

"Don't worry, she's like that with everyone. At least, every-one with a dog. She's got twenty-two cats living with her in that house."

Jack pinches his nose. "Euww."

The man gives another wave and walks on. But Elly's words still ring in your ears. "You'll never see Joe again." It can't be true, you tell yourself. It just can't be.

∃

THEDOGBYTES.COM

You join Jack and Tina after school in the computer lab. That's where you can usually find Jack anyway, helping the computer teacher Mr. Purdue configure a system.

Jack's seated in front of a monitor. "What was the name of that dog web site?" he asks you.

"You mean TheDogBytes.com?"

"Right. The one where you posted a notice about Joe being lost." He navigates over to it.

"There's one little page where humans are allowed to post messages, but otherwise it's all written by dogs," you explain.

Jack grunts. "Yeah. Right."

You shrug. It's funny, and a little bit uncanny. The site really does look as if it's run by canines. The home page shows a drawing of a dog with its teeth bared and its hackles raised.

TheDogBytes
For dogs only, by dogs only
Where we can share information, speak our secret thoughts, and be ourselves.
So roll in some mud, bark at anything you want, and leave your mark.
Humans Beware!

Jack clicks through some more pages. Sprinkled through-out are drawings of dogs in action. They're not the cute dog pictures people usually put on web sites. Instead, they show dogs doing what dogs like to do: rolling in a mud puddle, leaping for a rabbit's throat, lifting a leg on a mailbox.

Randy comes into the room and joins you. You tell him what you're looking at. "Read some of the messages the dogs have posted," you suggest.

Jack finds the main message board and clicks on some messages at random.

There's some very good trash in the alley between 6th and 7th streets. Happy hunting. —Hotbreath

Toffee has been taken away from us. She is at the dog pound now. We all know who did it. The human who was supposed to love her. The one who bought her in the first place. Her owner. Sure, Toffee had some quirks. But did she deserve to be thrown away like this? Someone should do something about that owner. —Sonya

Can somebody please explain these creatures that the humans serve? They own the city. They force humans and dogs and everyone else to stay out of their way—or else! The humans are swallowed up by them, then taken wherever the creature wants to go. Humans are their servants, washing and polishing and feeding them. These creatures have a terrible roar and an unnatural smell. Their four legs are circular and they can run faster than any dog. This must be the reason they hold supremacy. Can they be subdued? —Pup66

Howwwl-lo! This howl is for all dogs who are fed up with human behavior. There's a place you can go to escape. It's called Dog Wood, the only place where dogs are free. Join us. Many are coming. —Wolf8

Tina chuckles as she reads. "Kind of makes you see things in a different way, huh? Like maybe there's a lot going on in the dog world that we don't know about."

"Like Dog Wood," you say. "I wonder what that is."

"Huh," is all Randy replies, reading over your shoulder. "Hey, check out the Replies section. Maybe we got a reply to our post about Joe."

Jack clicks the Replies and you begin reading a series of posts that respond to previously asked questions.

To Rufus:
Well, once you've got it cornered, you've got two choices. It's either going to scratch you in the nose, in which case you will yelp and run away. Or, you can eat it. —Lickitup

To Hotbreath:
Thanks! I found half a pizza in the alley and ate the box, too. —Sarge

To Pup66:
I have been swallowed up by one of these creatures, but lived to tell the tale. It kidnapped me to the
vet! The only way they can be destroyed is if two of
them smash into each other. Then they are dead
and get taken away. —Sugar

"There's the reply to you, Randy," you announce, pointing farther down the list. "I used your screen name, Goal14."

To Goal14:
I'm not lost, Randy. I just don't want to be around
you any more. I'm sick of your abuse. Please stop
looking for me. I'm happy now. —Joe

You stare at Randy in stunned silence. His face crumples for a moment. But then he forces a smile. "Ha ha. That's a good one. I guess it proves how lame this web site is."

"But," Tina sputters, "how would they know your real name? We only gave them your screen name."

Randy remains resolute. "I don't know. They must have found it out through the Internet."

"It's possible," Jack says. "But nontrivial. Actually, it's kind of unlikely, come to think of it."

Suddenly a frightened look comes over Randy's face. "Wait a minute. What if it is from Joe? I mean, not really from *him*, but from someone who's taken him. Maybe he's not *lost* at all!"

You nod slowly. "Could be. Someone who already knows who you are."

Tina gapes at you. "Joe? Dognapped?"

"Or," you counter, "it might just be a hoax. The Internet is full of them."

"True, too true," Jack agrees.

Randy breathes a sigh. "We should go to the dog pound. Maybe we're worrying about nothing. Maybe that dog catcher Dooley picked him up, and Joe's just sitting there in the pound wondering what the heck's going on."

"Yeah, let's go," you agree.

"Okay," Jack says. "But do you want to reply to this person pretending to be Joe?"

Randy's eyes narrow with determination. He nudges Jack out of the chair and sits at the keyboard. Hitting the REPLY button, he types:

> To "Joe," i.e., the person who has him:
> You are sick. Whoever you are, return Joe immediately. If you don't give him back at once, I will go to the police. And, so help me, you better not hurt him. —Randy

Randy slams the SEND key, then stands up. "Let's go to the pound. If he's not there, I want to go back up to Portola Grove."

* * *

The dog pound is in a weedy neighborhood on the outskirts of town, near the small airport. It's an area of pawn shops, secondhand furniture, used car lots, and other discards. A starburst sign on a tall pole announces *Crescent Bay Dog*

Pound. The building looks like an old hangar that's been converted to its present use.

There's no bike rack, so you park and lock your bikes at the pole. Randy leads the way through the front door. As soon as he opens it, a din of dog voices resounds from somewhere in back. A sheet of drywall has been thrown up to create a front office.

A woman in a brown pantsuit sits behind a formica desk. She ignores you for a long minute. Then she removes her glasses, letting them dangle from a chain, and stares at you.

"Uh, I lost my dog," Randy explains. "I wanted to find out if maybe he got picked up . . ."

"Name?"

"His name's Joe, he's a black—"

"*Your* name."

"Randy Rivers. But how would you know—"

"He's got tags, right?"

Randy looks down at his sneakers. "No, that's the problem," he admits. "His collar wasn't on."

The woman lets out a disgusted sigh. She presses an intercom. "Mr. Norris?" she says. "A boy here with no tags."

"It'll be a minute, Tricia," the intercom replies.

She puts her glasses back on and ignores you. The four of you sit uneasily in fiberglass chairs. Jack mumbles something about government employees.

Tricia hears Jack's comment and glares at him. "This is a *private* business, sonny. Maybe you're too young to remember. The city turned over running the pound to us, Animal Services Unlimited. And we can kick you out of here any time we want."

Jack opens his mouth and then shuts it again. You hear

24

voices from behind a door. A few minutes later the door opens.

"This is an outrage," a man with a refined voice is saying. "I don't care if your resources are scarce. Dooley can't be treating our dogs like this, Mr. Norris."

As three figures emerge from the small office, you see that the man speaking is tall. He wears a houndstooth jacket and carries a big umbrella. A girl about your age is with him. She has a pony tail and is wearing a long fancy coat.

"Mr. Crossley, I do the best I can. But we're a business contracted by the city to control dogs. Like in any other business my boss wants me to watch the bottom line. We can't spend money we don't have."

"That's all dogs mean to you—money!" the girl accuses. "You don't care about animals at all!"

"We do, we do," Norris insists. "We're just a little short of staff. I admit it might take us a little bit longer than it should to notify owners that their pets have been found."

"If that's so, then Dooley shouldn't catch so many dogs," Crossley thunders. "You obviously can't handle them. Quit using money as your excuse!"

Norris raises his eyes to the ceiling. Instead of answering her, he addresses the father. "And tell me, how much money do *you* make on the dogs you breed?"

Crossley takes the girl's arm. "Come, Christina." He opens the door to leave, then stops and shakes his umbrella at Norris. "You'll be hearing from us again!"

All the air seems to go out of Mr. Norris as the door slams shut again. He rubs his eyes, then notices the four of you. "What's the problem?" he asks in a weary voice.

Randy explains about Joe. Norris folds him arms. "There's only one thing we can do," he says. "You'll have to look through all the dogs we have. See if yours is here."

Randy nods. Mr. Norris leads the way through a set of locked double doors, and then another set. The rest of you follow. From the way his shoulders slump, you can tell he's overworked.

When you go through the second set of doors, you're hit by an overwhelming roar. Barks, yips, and whines reverberate through the giant space, one on top of another. Hundreds of dogs are in here, locked in rows of cages.

As Norris leads you down the first row, you become aware of the smell, too. It's not just dogs, a smell you normally don't mind. There's something else. Fear. Anxiety.

"Where'd you lose the dog?" Norris asks Randy.

"Portola Grove," he answers. "I hear it's patrolled by a dog-catcher named Dooley."

"Yes, Dooley. Dooley, Dooley, Dooley."

For a minute you think Norris is losing his mind. You and Randy exchange a baffled look.

"What about him?" Randy asks tentatively.

"He's just . . . Dooley. People complain, but what can I do?"

Norris almost seems to be asking for your advice. His voice is so tired that none of you press him for more information about Dooley. Instead, you just continue down the row.

You look at each dog in its cage. Each eager, or pleading, or scared, or just plain listless face gazes back at you. Then you stop looking at them. You can't take it any more.

When you get to the end of the first row, Randy and Norris round the corner to inspect the next one. But you notice that Tina and Jack have stopped a few cages back. You wonder what they're doing down there, but decide you ought keep Randy company.

After several more rows of cages, Randy's shoulders slump. You've seen all the dogs. Joe is not here.

"Sorry," Norris comments. "Where are your friends? I need to close up."

"They're down here," you say, heading back to the first row.

Tina is crouched in front of a cage. As you draw closer, you hear her cooing to the dog inside. The dog looks young, not yet two years old. Her coat is gray. Not a dull gray, but a rich kind of gray that contains many colors.

She gives Tina's face a lick, but then backs off again. Even though Tina is doing all the gushing, the dog has eyes only for Jack.

"She's sooo cute!" Tina says. "What is she?"

"Mutt," Norris answers. "Her name's Mara."

"Kind of like the Spanish word for the sea," Randy notes. "Her coat is sort of that color. The sea on an overcast day."

"But her eyes are the green of the sea on a sunny day," Tina observes.

Norris suddenly lifts his hand to his mouth to cover a yawn. You know he wants to leave. But you linger for a minute, looking at Mara. Her face isn't like the others. In fact, you'd swear that the look on her face is an expression of love. And it's fixed on Jack.

Reluctantly the four of you turn and follow Norris back into the front office. "Will you let us know if someone brings in a black spaniel with no tags?" Randy asks.

"I'll try," Norris says, pausing at the door to his office. "But it might be better if you call me to follow up."

❊ ❊ ❊

27

The mood is glum as the four of you unlock your bikes. The pound, with all its doomed dogs, was an emotionally draining experience.

You get on your bikes and begin to ride slowly and aimlessly through the empty lots of the neighborhood.

Tina has been watching Jack the whole time. Suddenly she blurts, "She's crazy about you, Jack."

Jack just snorts.

"You know who I'm talking about," Tina persists. "She couldn't take her eyes off you."

"Dogs don't have emotions," Jack states.

"Do you?" Tina shoots back.

Jack flinches. "Let's keep our focus on our mission. We have to find Joe."

You make a little detour to avoid some broken glass in an abandoned lot. As you do, something catches your eye. You ride over to get a closer look.

What caught your attention is a familiar symbol on the crooked metal door of a small, crumbling stucco building. You circle the one-story building, but there are no windows.

The others have stopped and are looking at you. You wave them over. "Come here!"

They ride over. You point at the sign embossed on the door. "Whooaaa," Tina says slowly. "The snarling dog emblem from TheDogBytes.com."

"I think we should check it out," you say. "Maybe we can find out who sent that e-mail that was supposed to be from Joe."

The others nod, but stay on their bikes. You take a deep breath, get off your bike, and walk up to the door.

At first you knock lightly. When there's no answer, you knock harder. The door gives way under your knuckles.

"It's unlocked!" you say.

Tina jumps off her bike. "Yeah? Well, open it!"

Jack, you notice, is still on his bike, ready to flee at a moment's notice. Cautiously, you push the door open.

"Hello?" you call out. "Anybody here?" You take a step inside. It's dark. But when your eyes adjust to the light, you're surprised at what you see.

You poke your head out and motion for the others to join you. "Come on! I think we should investigate this place."

"All right!" Tina agrees.

But Randy gives you a good-bye wave. "Tell me what you find. But I need to go up to the Portola Grove neighborhood and look for Joe before it gets dark."

"Okay, good luck," you reply.

You brought the JackPack with you, of course. It contains all the tools you need. You shrug it off your back. As Jack joins you and Tina, you begin to investigate what appears to be the headquarters for TheDogBytes.com.

 Begin your investigation on the
Digital Detectives web site:

http://www.ddmysteries.com
and enter the key phrase **DOGBYTES**

When you've finished the investigation, the
web site will give you a page number to
return to.

Jack gets a panicked look on his face. "What's that sound?"

"It's a truck," you answer. "The guy on the phone is here already!"

"Let's get out of here!" Jack exclaims.

"No time!" Tina says. "We've got to hide!"

"Quick, under the table," you command.

The three of you crowd under the table in the second room. You have to squash in tight together. The guy will only find you if he looks behind the beat-up tablecloth.

The door swings open. "What's going on here?" the gruff voice bellows. You hear a pair of heavy boots walk around the first room. Then they come into the room. You hold your breath, along with Tina and Jack. All three of you tremble with fear.

"Boy, somebody's going to be in big trouble," the voice grumbles. The boots pause right in front of you. It wouldn't take much to reach out and grab them. Of course, that's the last thing on your mind.

Then, miraculously, the man leaves. The door slams behind him. You hear the truck start up and drive away. Finally you're able to breath a sigh of relief.

Tina is the first out from under the table. "Come on, let's finish this investigation," she says briskly.

Return to the Digital Detectives web site to do some more investigation:

http://www.ddmysteries.com
and enter the key phrase **FINISHDB**

When you've finished the investigation, the web site will give you a page number to return to.

4
CORRECT BEHAVIOR

You call Randy after dinner. You need to tell him about your investigation of the clubhouse, but mostly you want to ask if he had any luck finding Joe. You really hope he's been successful. Every day that Joe is missing, you feel worse.

"No," he says quietly. "I rode all over Portola Grove until after it was dark. No one has called, either."

"I'm really, really sorry, Randy," you say. "I feel so bad about this . . ."

There's a long pause on the phone. Finally, you think, Randy is going to let you have it. You almost wish he would. It only makes you feel more guilty when he's so heroic about it.

Instead, you hear him swallow deeply and say, "Don't worry. It could happen to anyone. That could have been me out there, letting Joe play. You can't watch him every single minute. I never did."

"Yeah, I guess . . ." Your voice trails off. Then you move onto the next tricky subject. "Do you really think Joe has been kidnapped?"

"Jack and Tina both called me and told me about the clubhouse," he answers. "There are some suspicious things. Like, how did the person who posted that reply to me know my name? And why won't the TheDogBytes people identify themselves?"

"Maybe it's just because they want you to think it's just dogs."

"Jack has been trying to trace the message that supposedly was from Joe. He can't find anything. Whoever sent it has covered their tracks well."

"Hmm." You think for a minute. "There's one thing, though—we took off Joe's collar. So if he's just lost, and someone found him, that could also explain why you haven't gotten a call. They might not have seen the posters."

"That's true," Randy allows. "I hope you're right. But meanwhile, I want to keep investigating TheDogBytes.com."

"Definitely," you agree. "But shouldn't we also go back to the park? We never interviewed potential witnesses there."

"You're right. Let's go after school tomorrow—wait, shoot, I have soccer practice. Well, maybe I'll skip it."

"Okay. We found that receipt from Connie's Pet Shop, too. We could visit them."

"Good idea." There's a pause. Randy's voice becomes a little lower and softer. "And thanks. I really appreciate how you guys are coming through for me."

Your throat tightens. You know you wouldn't have to be coming through on the search if you hadn't lost Joe in the first place. "We'll find Joe. We won't let you down."

You put down the phone. You hope with all your heart that you can live up to your promise.

* * *

The next afternoon, you ride with Tina up to Portola Grove park. Randy decided that he better check in with his soccer coach, so he says he'll meet you there. Jack also plans to meet you there later, though he's mysterious about why he couldn't just come with you.

The weather is back to being nice. There are a few scalloped clouds scooting high in the sky, but mostly it's a brilliant blue, like the ocean below. You get a great view of both from the park. People are gathered at the soccer field for a match between two girls' teams. Over at the dog run, the weather has brought out a big crowd of dogs and their walkers.

The people stand in knots, talking and watching their dogs. The dogs gather in clusters, too, sniffing, jumping, and playfully woofing. Every once in a while two dogs break out of a pack and go racing after each other.

You walk your bikes toward the group. A woman comes prancing in your direction, calling after her full-size poodle. "Leona, don't you love your momma? Come here."

Leona is sniffing around. As soon as her owner gets within a few feet, she gazes at her disdainfully, then moves off to a another group of dogs. She crosses your path, and the owner does too, calling, "Now come on, come to momma. Ooh, she loves you so much."

You and Tina have to stop abruptly to let the woman pass. Her sweet expression suddenly shifts to a look that could kill. "Stupid mutt," she mutters as she passes you.

As you approach another group, a brown Lab looks up and suddenly charges you. You and Tina freeze and hide behind your bikes. They're what seem to upset the dog. He snarls and barks at the pedal. You're afraid he might puncture a tire.

A man with a puffy face and messy black curls laughs and calls to the dog. "Don't worry, he's just got a thing about bikes. I don't know why, they just make him crazy!"

You approach slowly, keeping your bike between you and the dog. The man seems to think it's all very cute. Another man in the group says, "You never know what will set them off. Once my Gordon took a dislike to a UPS guy's tracking computer. The guy dropped it and Gordon just demolished the thing!"

Everyone laughs. Tina rolls her eyes at you. To these people, it seems their dogs can do no wrong.

"That's nothing," a woman relates. "My dog can read price tags. When I go out, she can tell which leather purse or new pair of shoes is the most expensive. That's the one she chews to bits, of course."

"Don't buy leather then," comes a serious voice. It belongs to Molly, who's in her beret again. The others look at her, then turn away. Tina waves hello. Molly returns a little smile.

"I've got a Great Dane that can't resist books," someone else says. "If we're in a cafe, he'll go take them right off someone's table. You should see their faces!"

This brings more laughter. A man passing by comments to the girl with him, "That's probably how they raise their children, too." He says it loud enough for everyone else to hear. "Without discipline or concern for how their behavior affects others."

As the others stare after him, Molly circles around to talk to you. "It's true," she murmurs. "These people have a human-centric view of dogs. They think they're just another form of entertainment. They don't know how to take their dogs' problems seriously."

You're still watching the man who just passed. "That was the guy at the pound," you say to Tina. "Mr. Crossley, and his daughter Christina."

"And their prize-winning Irish setter," Molly adds. "He's even worse than these other people. At least they don't turn their dogs into merchandise, like Crossley does."

"You mean he's a breeder?" Tina asks.

"Yes," Molly replies. "I don't know what he's doing down here, though. He usually trains his dog at the Highlands Kennel Club."

"Say," Tina says, "have you seen any sign of our dog Joe?"

"The one with the clipped tail? No, I'm sorry."

Just then Randy comes riding up behind you. "Hey!" he says. "Anyone heard anything?"

"No luck so far," Tina replies. She introduces Randy to Molly, who gives him a curt nod, then turns to one of her dogs.

You point out Crossley and Christina to Randy, and ask if he wants to go talk to them.

"Sure," he replies. The two of you take off, leaving Tina with Molly.

Mr. Crossley and his daughter have set up a series of hurdles on a small rise, apart from the other dog walkers. Crossley stands back with his arms folded. Christina puts the dog through its paces. The setter jumps over the hurdles, stops, turns, and sits. It's an impressive show. The dog has a regal bearing and is much better behaved than the others. Its trimmed coat is perfect. Everything it does is perfect. And yet it looks like it's having not one little bit of fun.

"Hello, Mr. Crossley," Randy hails. "We saw you at the pound yesterday. Can we ask a question? I lost my dog Joe up here, and I wonder if you've seen him."

Crossley makes a slight turn in Randy's direction. "I'm terribly sorry to hear that. What breed?"

"Cocker spaniel, a black one."

"Popular choice," he sniffs. He looks up, calls his daughter over, and introduces her. "Christina, have you seen a cocker, black, on the loose?"

"No, father." She turns her gaze to you. Her eyes are ice blue. Her hair, pulled back in a pony tail, is as perfectly coiffed as her dog's. She wears tiny gold earrings. "Have you been to the pound?"

"Uh, yeah," Randy says. "We saw you there, actually—so, what brought you down there?"

"It's that Dooley." Christina sighs. "We think he took one of our dogs again. He's so gross."

"So you have a missing dog, too?"

Crossley nods. "The man is too much. Far too zealous about his job. As a matter of fact, we've demanded a hearing about it."

Christina's dog rolls over on his back and starts to roll in the grass. Christina's face suddenly goes hard, and her voice lashes out like a whip. "Redley, bad! Bad! You stop that this instant!"

Redley gets to his feet at once. He cowers beneath her raised finger, his ears drooping to his toes. She smiles sweetly at you. "He needs a little correction now and then."

"It's all the bad influences around him," Crossley comments.

Randy looks at the man. "I guess you usually go to the kennel club. Why did you decide to come to the park today?"

Crossley frowns. "I don't see what business that is of yours. Yes, I use the kennel club when I please. Or not, when I please. You're not a member."

His statement doesn't leave much room for further response, so you just thank him and move on. You're heading back toward Tina and the others when you notice a plump figure entering the park.

Randy squints. "Is that—?"

"Satellite Jack," you finish for him. "And . . ."

"There's someone with him."

You watch Jack walk toward Tina, then you race down to join them. All of you converge at the same time. Tina gapes at Jack. Then at the leash in his hand. Then at the dog at the other end of the leash.

"It's Mara!" she squeals. "From the pound!"

"Sit, Mara," Jack commands.

Mara sits. She regards Jack with her gray-orange ears pricked alertly, head slightly tilted. Jack cocks his head, too. "The top of her left ear always stays folded over," he explains. "I don't know what it would take to make it stand up."

Tina puts her hands on his shoulders and jumps up and down. "You did it! You did it!"

Jack acts nonchalant. "Well, *somebody* had to feed her. And walk her. And I live pretty close to the park . . ."

Tina punches him in the shoulder. "See? You're in love too."

Jack tsks. "That is so inappropriate. We're dog and owner, that's all."

But he contradicts his words as soon as he kneels to take off her leash. He looks deep into her eyes. "I'll let you play with the other dogs. But you have to promise not to run off, okay? Just go play a while, and be careful."

Mara actually seems to understand him. She licks his nose, then bounds over to a clutch of dogs. You and Randy grin at each other.

"She's very smart," Jack announces.

"Naturally," you say.

"I think she has a good sense of language. I'm already teaching her some words. There are, it seems, cases of dogs who can read written language."

"Sheez, Jack, you sound like you're programming a computer," Tina remarks. "Or conducting an experiment."

Jack looks hurt. He avoids her eyes as he replies, "I just want her to be able to tell me what she wants."

Tina puts a hand on his shoulder again. "Don't worry, Jack. You'll know."

You all watch Mara approach a couple of dogs. Though one is just a toy poodle, Mara still keeps her tail and head low. She allows the poodle to sniff her, and the other dog as well. She even rolls over and shows them her stomach.

Jack gives a running commentary of Mara's behavior. "See, Mara's the youngest," Jack explains. "Even though she's bigger, she'll submit to the older dogs and follow their example. She wants to learn, fit in."

"You've been doing some research, Jack," you say.

"Dogs have their own rules," Randy comments. "They know how to act with one another. Most of the time."

"Yeah, they're more reliable than people," Jack answers. "And more honest."

You wonder if that's why Jack is so taken by this dog. He may be able to decipher the innards of a computer, but human behavior baffles him. And with his parents and older sister so distracted by their own projects, Mara will always pay attention to him at home.

"Just keep an eye on her," Randy comments.

Jack nodded. "I put a chip in her collar. It has a transmitter that will allow me to home in on her. Plus, if someone who finds her happens to interface her with an infrared port, I've written a program that will automatically give them all her information, plus e-mail me that she's been found."

Tina bursts out laughing. But Randy says, "Cool."

"I'll make one for Joe," Jack offers. "That is, if . . ."

You all gaze down at your shoes as you remember the reason that brought you to the park in the first place.

"Uh, find out anything from that guy Crossley?" Tina asks Randy.

Randy shakes his head. "He's a breeder. Belongs to the Highlands Kennel Club. You find anything?"

"Nothing," Tina replies glumly.

Randy slams a fist into his palm. "We're getting nowhere!"

You're startled by his sudden outburst. But you can understand it. He must feel pretty frustrated by now.

The conversation is interrupted by the sound of a woman yelling. It's Molly. With each sentence she screams, she bounces on tiptoe, rising up over a man with thinning blond hair and a suede leather jacket.

"Never hit a dog! Do you hear me? You have no right!"

The man shrinks away from her, holding up his hands. "Okay, okay, I won't do it again," he says.

Molly isn't satisfied, though. She slaps his arm twice. "How do you like it, huh? How do you like it? You don't deserve that dog."

The man stoops to pick up a leash, then flees.

"Bully!" Molly calls after him.

She waits until he's far away, then turns to look at a friend of hers near the edge of the woods, a man with bushy chestnut-blond hair. Your eyes travel up the hill above them, where you notice Crossley and Christina standing, each with their arms folded in the exact same way, taking in the scene.

"Molly's kind of intense," you note.

"Yeah, she really *really* cares about dogs," Tina says. "She told me some stuff that really made me think about how we treat animals. I think I'm going to stop eating meat."

To no one's surprise, Jack finds a flaw in her logic. "But animals eat meat. We're animals. Where's the problem?"

"You can get all the protein you need from vegetable foods," Tina says, obviously quoting Molly.

"I'm not arguing that," Jack replies. "All I'm saying is, she thinks animals are so great. Animals don't feel all guilty about eating meat. So why can't we be like them?"

Tina throws up her arms. "We'll go to a slaughterhouse some time, okay? Molly said she'd take me. You come with us, and then decide if you still want to eat meat."

"I can handle it," Jack declares.

Your attention is distracted by another little conflict. Two dogs have faced off, growling at each other. It looks as if they're about to fight. The owners stand tensely by, appealing to their dogs to calm down.

One dog advances. Then, as quickly as it began, the altercation ends. The other dog lowers its ear and its tail and waits submissively for the first one to sniff it.

"They just had to establish who's alpha," Jack explains. "Once they know who's dominant, they can be friends."

"Doesn't the other dog feel bad?" you wonder.

"Not really. It matters more to figure out where they are in the hierarchy. Once they all know, everyone's happy."

No sooner do the two dogs start playing than a boy's voice cries out. It's a kid about six years old. "Where's my puppy!" he screams. "My puppy is gone!"

People gather around him, trying to help. Someone points

toward the parking lot. There you see a big truck labeled Crescent Bay Dog Pound.

"Dooley's here!" an adult declares.

"It's Dooley! He did it!" someone else agrees.

You expect to see them run over to the truck to confront him. But no one takes a step in that direction. They all seem to be afraid of the dog catcher. The kid stares at the truck, then turns away in tears.

Randy tugs at your sleeve. "Come on. This is our chance to question Dooley. Everybody keeps talking about him."

You start walking toward Dooley's truck, though you're a little nervous doing so. You turn back to see if Tina is coming too, but she's still debating with Jack. "Do you know what kind of chemicals they pump into cows?" you hear her say as you walk off.

"Tina, take care of our bikes, okay?" you call to her.

You feel as if everyone in the park is watching you as you stalk over to confront the dog catcher who might be behind all your troubles. Randy strides right up and knocks on the passenger door.

It opens. Inside is a man in his thirties, wearing blue overalls. He's got a big chest, a round belly, and giant hands. He glares at you from sunken eyes. "Yeah?"

"Can we talk to you?" Randy asks earnestly. "My dog is missing."

"Yours and everyone else's," Dooley comments warily. "And you all think it's my fault."

"He's a black cocker spaniel—" Randy begins.

Dooley puts up a hand to stop him, then motions you into the truck. "Look, you can talk to me. I got nothing to hide. But I got work to do, too."

Randy goes up the first step of the truck. You tap him on the back. When he turns, you mouth the words, "Is this okay?"

Randy nods. "We've got to find Joe!" he whispers.

You hesitate another moment, remember your role in losing the dog, and then follow. The door closes behind you with a rush of air and the truck roars off.

5

WHOSE BEST FRIEND?

The dog catcher's truck lurches out of the Portola Grove parking lot. Dooley's big arms crank the wheel with ease. Randy sits in the passenger seat. You crouch in a small space behind him, gripping the back of the seat for balance. As Dooley turns onto a street, you hear animal nails sliding across metal in the back of the truck. You take a look. Dooley has three dogs in small cages, though none of them are puppies. Maybe he didn't take that little boy's dog after all.

Dooley stares straight ahead. His face is like a mask, but you can sense a troubled presence underneath. His skin is pockmarked. His hair is long and a bit oily. When he turns his head a little, you notice creases of dirt around his ears.

"So how's it going?" Randy ventures.

Dooley grunts. A small choking sound comes from his throat, then he clears it with a giant hawk, rolls down his window, and spits. "Scuse me."

Randy decides to get back to business. "My dog Joe disappeared from Portola Grove two days ago. He's a black cocker spaniel. Have you seen him?"

"So what'd you do to lose him?"

"It was my fault," you volunteer, hoping it'll make Dooley nicer to Randy. "I had him in the park, and we accidentally took off his collar, and suddenly he was gone."

"You people don't know how to live with dogs," Dooley replies. "Most kids shouldn't be allowed to have dogs. At all."

This is not going well. You have an urge to ask Dooley to let you out of the truck right now. You glance at the rearview mirror and you're startled to see Dooley's small dark eyes pinned on you. He's watching your reaction.

You try to rise to the occasion. "Well, what about all those dogs who need homes? Our friend Jack just adopted a dog named Mara from your pound."

Dooley's head jerks up and he gives you a sharp mirror glance. Air hisses from his mouth. "Mara, huh? He'd better be good to her. That's all I can say."

It's clearly a threat. You make a note to warn Jack.

"So, about Joe," Randy resumes.

"Haven't seen him," Dooley answers abruptly.

"Are you sure?" Randy pushes.

Now Randy is the target of Dooley's eyes. "Look buddy, *you* let him get lost. Don't blame *me*." He shakes his head. "And don't blame Joe, either. Ninety-nine percent of the time, it's the owner's fault."

Dooley slams on the brakes. You're pressed into the back of Randy's chair.

"Heyyyy, Kiki!" Dooley cries to a husky trotting down the sidewalk. Amazingly enough, the dog seems to say hello back. It stops and lifts its head to the truck, tongue hanging out, tail high. Dooley grins, waves, and then begins to drive on.

"So you're not going to pick him up?" you ask as you recover your balance.

"Her," Dooley corrects you. "And, no."

He stops the truck again so you can observe the dog. "See,

there's a dog that knows what she's doing. She's going to cross the street now. See how she pauses and listens for cars?"

You watch Kiki do just as Dooley says. "Now she'll go over and check out the dog across the street," he goes on. "But she never causes trouble. She's just being social. They're social animals, you know? I feel sorry for dogs in big cities. It's terrible to leave them locked up alone by themselves all day. People get them because they feel isolated in the urban environment. They want a dog for a companion. Except then they leave the dog by itself all day long in a tiny apartment while they go to work. That can eat a dog up. It's criminal."

"At least they rescue them from the pound," you say.

Dooley stares stonily ahead. "Sometimes. If that's where they get the dog, then okay. An apartment is better than the alternative. But half of those people, they're such snobs, they buy their dogs. They want some special breed."

"I guess you don't like purebreds?" Randy comments.

"Hey, nothing against the dogs." Dooley puts the truck in gear and starts to drive on. "It's the breeders. I could just—" his giant hands make a mangling motion. "They create this nonsense. A few purebreds, that's okay. But it's a mania with these people. Look at all the resources that go into it. All the effort and care, all the money to create these hoity-toity dogs, when there are already so many good dogs without homes. It *disgusts* me."

His face is red. You try to think of something good to say about breeders, but Dooley interrupts you. "Plus, purebreds have all kinds of problems. They get weird ailments because their body structure gets contorted to produce a certain

47

look. If some dogs have to be destroyed somewhere—believe me, I wish they didn't—but if they do, it should be those freaks. Not the healthy mixes."

You're left a little breathless by Dooley's tirade. Randy tries to return to the main subject by asking, "So how do you decide which dogs to pick up and which ones not to?"

"Simple," he answers. "There's a difference between dogs who know what they're doing and ones that don't. I only pick up the ones that don't, because their owners are careless enough to put them in danger."

He checks his watch. "I'll give you an example." He puts the truck into high gear, makes a couple of turns, and comes to a bus stop. A beagle is sitting there patiently. "This dog comes to the bus stop every day at this time. You know why? His master used to come home from work on this bus. His master died two years ago. The dog lives with the widow, but he still comes to the bus stop every day. When the next bus comes, he'll go home. This dog knows what he's doing."

"But what's so bad about a dog that's just wandering—" you begin.

"Do you know how many dogs are killed by cars every year in this town?" Dooley bursts out. "You know how many dead dogs, injured dogs, I pick up every month? It makes me *sick*."

His knuckles are white as he grips the steering wheel. "And you know what I've been finding lately around Portola Grove? Dogs who've died of starvation. Can you imagine that? So yeah, I'll pick up a dog for its own good. But it's the owners I'd like to lock up. There are no bad dogs, just bad owners."

"I see," Randy comments.

Dooley gives him a sidelong glance. "Do you?"

"Yeah," Randy responds. "There are two sides to it."

"Most people don't," Dooley says. "If you really do see, you can come down to City Hall for a hearing tomorrow night. It's supposed to be about dog control in Crescent Bay, but really it's because everyone's got it out for *me*."

"We'll come," Randy promises. A moment later, he adds, "Do you think you could take us back to the park?"

"The park?" Dooley exclaims. "No, look, I gotta work."

"Okay . . ." Randy says slowly. "Um, do you know where Connie's Pet Shop is? Maybe you could drop us there."

"Good thinking," you say to Randy. You found a receipt from Connie's in the clubhouse. Someone there might know something about TheDogBytes.com.

"I can do that. It's not too far," Dooley responds.

He steers the truck to Branch Avenue, the main commercial street in town. After pulling up in front of the shop, he opens the door to release you. As he does, he waves to someone inside.

Randy jumps out of the truck and thanks Dooley. You thank him, too, but you're preoccupied. Your mind is on Kiki, the dog Dooley talked about. The name rings a bell. Wasn't she one of the dogs who posted a message on the web site?

✳ ✳ ✳

You've never seen a pet shop like Connie's. At first you think it's a bakery. Laid out in trays in the front of the store are rows and rows of cookies: peanut butter ducks, frosted ginger cats, and carob squirrels. It makes you hungry, until you read the ingredients list. The cookies are for dogs. And they cost $1.50 each.

You and Randy wander around the store. "I never knew you could need so many things for your dog," he comments.

There are silk pillows and beds. There are fur paw and ear muffs. Nail files and clippers. Hair brushes, shavers, strippers, and other grooming tools you have no idea how to use. There's dog shampoo, detangler, and conditioner. A couple of perfumes, and even spritzers for your dog. Lots of fuzzy playthings, shaped as mice, cats, and rabbits. Endless choices of foods. And chew toys of every kind—hot dogs, chicken legs, Fudgesicles.

"Do dogs really care if their chew toy looks like a sushi roll?" you wonder.

"It's the owners who spend the money," Randy points out. "I guess you have to appeal to them."

The shop is very busy, so the store owner hasn't noticed you until now. She has long, straight, shiny black hair, pinned back with two pink bows. She flashes you a smile and says, "Hi, I'm Connie. So what do you need for that special dog in your life?"

Randy's face falls, as the fact of Joe's being lost hits him once again. You step in and say, "We're just kind of looking. Do you know about a hearing being held down at City Hall?"

"It's tomorrow night," a deep voice replies. It comes from a tall man with a white goatee and little bit of hair left on his head. His safari-style shirt dangles loose over his large stomach. He wears small wire spectacles which give him a friendly look.

"And the timing is terrible," he continues. "Don't those people know we've got a show coming up this weekend?"

"A dog show?" Randy asks.

"Bingo." The man squints, then holds out a well-manicured hand. "Houston Smith."

Randy shakes his hand and tells Houston both your names.

"The big county dog show is on Saturday," Connie explains. "It's held at the fairgrounds. Dogs come from all over the area. The Highlands Kennel Club will be showing all their best breeds."

Houston Smith beams. "So you must be a member," you guess. "Do you know Mr. Crossley?"

Houston's friendly look disappears. "Crossley! Why'd you have to go and ruin a perfectly nice conversation?"

"Poor Houston," purrs a woman coming down the aisle. Dark curls cascade over the collar of her black leather jacket. "I hear Crossley's afraid to show his face at the club any more."

"What did he do to you?" you ask Houston.

"Stole my bloodlines!" he thunders.

Connie introduces the new woman as Darwina Lopez, a veterinarian. Darwina gives you a smile. "Bertram Crossley is a rather sensitive subject with Houston," she explains.

"I'll get him back," Houston fumes. "I'll show him how it feels to lose a dog or three. Thief."

"Even Crossley wouldn't steal a dog," Darwina says.

"Oh no?" Houston counters. "Then explain this to me: why is it that his litter of nine-month-olds are the spitting image of my hound Grover?"

"Now Houston, you know you got Grover back," Darwina chides. "I'm sure he was just picked up by Dooley for a few days. Instead of worrying about Crossley, wouldn't it be better just to win best of breed at the show?"

"Sure," Houston grumbles. "But another dog of mine disappeared just last week. I talked to Dooley, and he's not the one. I want some answers."

"My dog is missing too," Randy puts in. "A black cocker spaniel named Joe. Has anyone has seen him?"

Connie, Darwina, and Houston all shake their heads. "I'm sorry," Connie says. "It seems like a lot of dogs are getting lost lately."

"Someone needs to get to the bottom of it," Houston says.

"I've always wondered about that genetic research lab out near Airport Road," Connie says. "Canigen Labs. They do research on dogs. It's terrible. They need a lot of dogs— where do they get them?"

When no one answers right away, you say, "Has anyone heard of TheDogBytes.com?"

Darwina chuckles. "It's amusing. A web site that appears to be written entirely by dogs."

"So you don't think it could have something to do with the lost dogs?" you say.

"I doubt it," Darwina answers. "But who knows what it's up to? Some of the dogs on the site seem pretty anti-human. You should check it out, Houston."

"Hmm, maybe." Smith rubs his stubble. "I still think Crossley is the one to blame for the missing animals. At least mine. He's up to something, that much I know."

Darwina pats his forearm. "You'll have your chance for revenge at the show."

Houston's mouth puckers. "Yeah, I'll beat him. This is war."

Darwina waves good-bye. "Well, I've got to go. See you there. Or maybe at the hearing tomorrow night."

Houston gives a chivalric bow. He grumbles a "nice to meet you" in your direction, then goes to inspect the variety of dog food in the back of the store.

"It's getting late," Randy says. "We'd better go, too."

You nod. "But we've got plenty to investigate. The hearing tomorrow night. The dog show on Saturday. It should be an interesting weekend."

* * *

During dinner, you tell your parents about the dog show, the kennel club, and Portola Grove. They're sorry to hear that Joe is still missing. Of course you can go to the hearing tomorrow night and the show the next day, they say.

After the meal, you polish off your homework as quickly as you can. Then you log on to the Internet and return to the dog web site. First you check the "new postings" page.

Bone bonanza! Behind the new eatery called Chicken Feed in the El Dorado mall. Just be careful when you chew. The bones splinter and you can choke on them. —Lickitup

Over here on 20th street, we keep hearing about dogs being lost. It's going on all over the city. I happen to know that Dooley is not to blame. Does anyone know what's up? —Chester

Interesting. You navigate over to see if there's a reply to this message. It turns out there's a whole string of them.

To Chester:
Why do humans say we are "lost" when they can't find us? We're just doing what we feel like doing. It's the humans who are lost. They have no ability to follow a scent. They have terrible hearing. They have no idea where we like to go. If they can't take the trouble to understand us, they ought to just leave us alone. —High Tail

To High Tail:
Well put. But I'm afraid the answer is not for the humans to leave us alone. They just need to pay closer attention. —Essie

To Essie:
I'm sorry, humans are nothing but a self-serving species. They don't care about dogs. All they care about is what we can do for them. Sit, fetch, be quiet. Do our business only when they let us out, and half the time they stand there watching us. When they need us, it's all "Come here, poochie, poochie." But when we need them, they act like we're bothering them. I've had enough. I'm high-tailing it to Dog Wood. —Red Ears

To Red Ears:
Yes, humans are self-serving. But all species act in their own interests. Dogs and humans can get

along, but humans must be educated to be less self-ish and thoughtless. We just need to teach them on how to live with us. —Chester

To Chester:
Fool! Humans have enslaved us for long enough. It's time to leave them behind. Break your chains! We can escape to Dog Wood. There are no limits on us there. We can be free, like our ancestors the wolves. —Wolf8

To Wolf8:
We do all have a little wolf in us. But dogs have always lived with humans. We can't return to our primal ancestors. We are not equipped for it. For better or worse, our fate lies with humans. —Sonya

To Sonya:
So long, stooge. You'll never amount to anything more than "man's best friend." —Red Ears

Wow. That's quite a heated discussion. These messages make it seem as if there's some kind of revolution going on in the dog world. You can practically hear the growls and snarls.

You scroll up to check other replies. Then you notice one that was posted last night.

It's a response to the message Randy sent to the person who had written pretending to be Joe. Randy had accused them of taking Joe and demanded they give him back.

To Randy:

Arrogant boy! Nobody's "holding" me. You think dogs can't do anything for themselves. You have a lot to learn. You had your chance, Randy, and now it's too late. Don't try to find me. I won't come back to you anyway. —Joe

You wonder if you should forward the message to Randy, in case he hasn't seen it. It's sure to upset him. But he'll be more upset if you don't tell him about it. You send on the message.

Then you sit back and stare out your darkened window. It's late now. Somewhere, a dog barks. You wonder what it's saying. An eerie feeling comes over you. It does almost seem as if the messages on the web site come from dogs themselves. You know it can't be true, but still, it gets you wondering. Do we really have any idea what goes on in dog's minds? Or do we only see what we want to see?

6

THE HEARING

You, Randy, and Tina crowd into a room in City Hall the following night. The place is packed. The hearing on dogs and dog catchers in the town of Crescent Bay is about to begin.

Jack tried to come inside with you, but he was turned away at the door because he had Mara. "No dogs allowed in City Hall," the guard told him.

Jack stared at the guard like she was a two-headed ogre. "You mean dogs can't even come to their own hearing?" Then he turned away, tugging on Mara's leash. "I guess we'll go for a walk. I'll meet you later."

"Jack doesn't usually make such faux *paws*," you commented after he left. "What got into him?"

Randy groaned at the pun. "Mara," Tina responded quickly. "He couldn't bear to be away from her for an evening."

You also noticed the sad look on Randy's face as he watched Jack and Mara walk away. There was nothing you could do but pat him on the back.

You had talked to him earlier in the day about the latest response from "Joe." Randy was about ready to take a sledgehammer to the TheDogBytes clubhouse. You'd never seen him so mad. You pointed out that the message could have come from someone using the web site, not necessarily the site itself.

But now Randy is back to his usual cool self as you settle into chairs in the hearing room. Two tables are up front, each equipped with a microphone. A city official in a gray suit sits in front of it. He introduces himself as Mr. Kuo. To his left is Mr. Norris, from the pound, and also Elly Shotte, the woman with twenty-two cats who objected to your putting up posters for Joe. To his right is Mr. Crossley, the breeder.

Kuo calls the meeting to order. He says that a number of people have demanded a hearing about the question of dogs and the management of the Crescent Bay Dog Pound.

"We have three citizens representing different viewpoints on the issue," Kuo says. "Mr. Norris, of course, runs the pound. Elly Shotte represents those who would like to see tighter control on dogs in the city. And Bertram Crossley is a member of the Highlands Kennel Club."

Mr. Norris goes first. He reminds the audience that several years ago the city decided to contract out the job of running the pound to a private firm, Animal Services Unlimited. "And in those years, we believe we have done a good job of managing dog control for the city," Norris says. "Ever year, we have stayed within our budget. Please keep in mind that as a private business, we will do things differently than a government agency. We have to watch our bottom line. This is a decision the people of the city made."

Elly Shotte gets to go next. She's in a lemon chiffon dress, more dressed up than when you first saw her. She folds her hands and regards the audience for a moment, making sure she has their full attention. "Too many dogs are allowed to run wild in this city," she says in a stern voice. "They dig up gardens, befoul trees, chase small animals, and in general are a nuisance."

Some people hiss and groan at her words, but others clap. "You tell them, Elly!" someone calls out.

Elly tosses her head and looks away, pretending like the other people in the room don't exist. When the room has quieted down, she finishes. "We made a mistake in turning over the control of dogs to a private enterprise. They need to think about the safety of our citizens first, not their bottom line. The only employee who is doing a good job is Dooley."

There are boos at the mention of his name. Kuo asks the crowd to refrain from such responses. Then he turns the mike over to Mr. Crossley.

Crossley is the only one who stands up. He takes a deep breath. "We are in a grave crisis," he declares. "Dogs are being taken from us left and right. Elly, in her twisted way, put her finger on the problem. We all know who it is. Dooley! He's out of control. He picks up a dog on his own whim, and then does who-knows-what with them."

Crossley shakes his head sadly, then continues. "It used to be that the pound would notify an owner if a dog was brought in. But now your dog might be put to sleep before you know it's even been picked up. Besides, who knows what Dooley really does with them. Maybe he never takes them to the pound. The situation is intolerable!"

This draws applause from the audience. Norris leans over to try to say something, but Crossley keeps the mike. His mouth is trembling. He shakes his fist at someone in the back of the room. "Just today, my daughter's valuable Irish setter disappeared. *What have you done with her, Dooley?*"

Heads turn to glare at a forlorn figure in the back. It's Dooley, still in his blue work suit. His shoulders slump. "I didn't pick up no setter today," he responds quietly.

"Oh, baloney!" Crossley yells. His face has flushed red. He grips the mike and scans the audience. "Who else is a victim of this man? Who else's dog is missing?"

You're amazed by the number of hands that are raised. Other people in the room are, too. A general gasp goes up. Dooley shrinks back into the shadows. In the meantime, Kuo manages to get the mike from Crossley. "Let's hear from some of you in the audience."

Houston Smith stands up and, with his big voice, over-rides anyone else's efforts to speak. "I agree there's a problem," he booms. "But let's not hand out blame too fast. I'm pretty sure Bertram Crossley is the one who put his hands on some of my dogs."

"That's a lie!" Crossley sputters. "How low can you sink, Houston?"

"Me sink?" Houston bellows back. "You're the one who hasn't won a best of breed in four years, so now you're taking other people's dogs. I'm *so* sorry your daughter's setter is gone. Maybe it's a little bit of justice."

Crossley gapes at him. "You did it, didn't you? You took Redley. Maybe you're going to sell him on the black market. I know you need the money."

"Cur!" Houston retorts.

To your surprise, Tina stands up next. "Maybe the dogs are leaving by themselves, like it says on TheDogBytes.com."

"What's that all about?" Kuo asks.

"I suggest you read it," Houston replies. "Someone is trying to make it appear as though our dogs are turning against us."

A buzz starts among the crowd. "Look at Elly," Tina whispers as she sits down again. Elly is sitting back with her arms folded, smug as a cat.

The buzz is finally quieted by Dooley's voice from the back. "Maybe dogs can run a web site, and maybe they can't. Either way, maybe you ought to make a better effort to understand them. They're trying to tell us something. What makes you think they like to be paraded around like little dolls at your shows?"

"Dogs are utterly and completely dependent on human beings," Crossley snaps. "All that they can tell us is exactly what we teach them."

"*That's* the problem!" This eruption comes from a guy wearing a big outdoors jacket, the guy you saw with Molly at the park. Molly is next to him. He leaps up dramatically to point at Crossley.

"My name is Mark Lupin," he says, "and I'm with the Animal Rights Force. I know a thing or two about dogs—for instance, they have telepathic powers. Maybe they really *can* run a web site. Maybe they really *are* rebelling!"

"Pshaw!" is all Crossley has to say to that. But you wonder about the telepathy idea. There are definitely times when it seemed as if Joe could read your mind.

"Look, Crossley," Mark goes on, "we're sick of your condescending attitude toward dogs. It's time you started treating your dogs right."

Crossley fixes Mark with his stone-like stare. "You obviously know nothing about breeders. *We're* the ones who keep the knowledge, passed down through generations, alive. *We're* the ones who know the breeds and their characteristics. We maintain diversity, so that the gene pool doesn't get all mixed up. Young man, I know and care for my dogs far better than you'll ever understand any animal that you claim to 'save.'"

Mark rakes a hand through his mop of chestnut brown hair. "You know what you are?" Mark responds. "Racial purists. Like the Nazis."

Crossley shakes his head and looks over at Kuo. "Honestly. Do we have to listen to this?"

Molly jumps up. "Yes, you do! We haven't even come to the real issues yet."

She spreads her hand and starts enumerating on her fingers. "Number one, when is the pound going to stop destroying dogs? It's a crime! Number two, when are we going to change the law to acknowledge that we are not 'owners of pets' but 'caretakers of animals'? They're not our slaves. And number three, when are we going to ban experiments on animals in Crescent Bay? It's happening right here under our noses at Canigen Labs."

At the mention of Canigen, a man in his late twenties stands up. His sun-streaked hair falls jauntily down over his collar. He wears a wool sweater, and speaks in a broad Australian accent. "Now wait a minute. My name is Peter Frost. I'm head of research at Canigen. And I can tell you that the work we're doing is very, very important."

"Important to the patent that will make you millions of dollars," Molly retorts. "How many dogs do you have at your lab, Peter?" She turns to the rest of the audience. "If you're wondering why so many dogs are missing, maybe you should investigate Canigen. These labs always need research subjects."

"That's an outrage!" Peter Frost cries.

Norris backs him up. "I can't believe that would happen."

"Believe it," Molly says. "It's happened before, on the East Coast. Professional dognappers steal dogs and sell them to middlemen, who sell them to medical researchers. It could happen here."

"Well, it's not," Frost states. "Not at Canigen."

"We'd like to believe you, Peter," says Molly. "I have a simple solution. Let us come and inspect your laboratory."

Frost throws up his hands. "You know that our research is secret. But I'll be glad to draw up a list of our dogs for you."

"Just how carefully do you screen the dogs you receive?" Darwina Lopez asks. "Is it possible you're getting stolen dogs without knowing it?"

"No chance." Frost tugs at a strand of hair. "Look, I know everyone is upset about their missing dogs. But I promise you, you're looking in the wrong place."

Crossley grabs the mike. "I agree with Mr. Frost. We've gone off track with all of this nonsense. I suggest we go back to what this hearing was about in the first place—Dooley."

"With all due respect, Mr. Crossley," Norris interrupts, "I don't think we've been off track at all. What we've been hearing tells me that Dooley and the pound are not the problem."

"Not so fast, Norris," Crossley declares. "The Dooley matter is far from resolved. Nor is the matter of your management of the pound. In fact, maybe we should hear from Mr. Dooley himself. What do you think about the way the pound is being run?"

All eyes turn to the rear of the room. Dooley's shoulders slump even more. He turns bashful in front of all these people. It's quite a contrast from his confident demeanor in the truck.

"Well, Mr. Dooley?" prompts Kuo.

Dooley ducks his head. "I just do my job. The pound is . . .

all right. I can't say any more. I don't want to get fired."

"You can speak freely," Norris assures him.

"It just needs more money!" Dooley bursts. "I worked for the city when it ran the pound. Then people voted not to give it enough funding. Now you're all here complaining. We just don't have enough manpower."

Crossley's face is like stone, boring into the nervous man. "On the contrary, I think you overuse your manpower. You're picking up a record number of dogs—you *must* be, or else where are they all going?"

"No!" Dooley wails. "I pick them up for their own good. Do you have any idea—I found two dogs dead of starvation on my route this week. And three more who nearly were. And others who were sick or lame. *What are you people doing?*"

"It's true," Darwina Lopez confirms. "We've seen more injured, sick, and hungry dogs in my clinic than usual. Well above average. Something is going on."

"There are too many dogs," Elly Shotte declares. "It's just natural selection."

Houston Smith stands up and flicks his fingers at Elly. "Why do we even listen to her?" he demands hotly. "She doesn't care about anything except cats."

Elly's fingers curl into claws. She jumps to her feet, eyes blazing. "Cat-hater!"

Houston licks his lips and a slow smile spreads across his face. "Aw, Elly, you know I love cats," he drawls. "They taste just like chicken."

Elly screams. A cacophony of jeers, hisses, and laughter fills the room. Houston sits down, delighted with himself. Darwina covers a smile. Mr. Kuo pounds the table for order.

"That's enough! I've made a decision," Mr. Kuo

declares. "The city will set up a committee to investigate the disappearances, illnesses, and so on. We'll hold a meeting to announce the members of the committee on Monday night."

A groan goes up from the people in the crowd who didn't get a chance to speak. Kuo appears to have had about enough for one night, but he does allow a woman in front to ask one more question.

"Aren't you going to report the missing dogs to the police?"

"I've spoken to the Chief already," Kuo responds. "He said he needs more than rumors and anecdotes to act. So if someone has some hard evidence, please give it to me. But thus far, this is not a matter on which the police are willing to spend their valuable time."

Darwina raises her hand to speak. After Kuo recognizes her, she announces, "Anyone who is missing a dog should come to my clinic to see some of the animals we've taken in. None of them have collars or tags."

"Very good," Kuo says. He surveys the room. "Now, that's it. This hearing is over."

A new chorus of complaints begins. Kuo holds up a finger. "And—I will accept written comments and complaints starting on Monday. The comments will be forwarded to the committee. If you have a message for Mr. Norris, Dooley, Canigen Labs, or anyone else, I'll copy it to them."

He unplugs the microphone and starts to pack his briefcase. Crossley is beside him, railing about something. Kuo appears serenely oblivious. Elly Shotte, still seated, is cradling a cat in her arms. You notice a large handbag by her feet. She must have smuggled it in.

Randy just stares straight ahead, frustration written all

over his face. Tina tugs at your sleeve. "I think someone wants to talk to us."

You look up. Christina Crossley is waiting at the end of the row. Another girl stands with her. Christina waves you over. "We hear you're detectives," she says in an earnest voice.

Her cool, clear, direct gaze never leaves you. You glance down at her fingers. The nails are lacquered clear. She radiates cleanliness. She's so perfect in every respect, she makes you nervous.

But she doesn't have the same effect on Tina. "Yeah, and?" Tina demands.

"We want to hire you to find our dogs." Christina zeroes in on you again. "You met Redley. You saw how wonderful he is. He'd never run away. Someone stole him, I'm sure of it. One of my dad's dogs disappeared earlier in the week, too. I don't know if Dooley did it. He's a creep, but I don't think he's that smart . . ."

"Do you have a suspect?" you ask.

Christina gives a petite shrug. "Not really. I just want Redley back. And Lindsay—this is my friend Lindsay—lost her dog too."

"He's a weimaraner," Lindsay says. She has shiny brown hair drawn back in a ponytail.

"You're also at the kennel club?" you ask her.

"Yes. We know a lot of people who've lost a dog."

"You mentioned a reward," Tina says. "How much?"

Christina glances nervously toward her father, who's now talking to Peter Frost. "My father can't know about this. He'd think I don't trust him to find Redley. But Lindsay and I have pooled our money. We might be able to get more from my mom."

Randy is standing behind Tina. He puts a hand on her shoulder. "Don't worry about the reward," he tells Christina. Ignoring Tina's dirty look, he goes on, "It's clear that very suspicious things are happening to dogs in this town. We're already investigating anyway. We'll try to find your dogs just like all the others. Including my own."

"We'll start at the dog show tomorrow," you put in.

Christina's face falls. "Oh. I was hoping—maybe—if I had him back for the show—"

Randy smiles indulgently. "We're not *that* good. It's already nine o'clock. We need a little more time."

Lindsay lowers her voice. "Do you think it's a dognapper?"

"It's hard to say," you reply. "We need to interview people. Gather evidence. Look for a pattern."

Christina does the little shrug again. "All right. Thank you." She pulls a couple of bills from a small jeweled purse. "We have a down payment . . ."

Randy prevents Tina from reaching for them. "Don't worry about it. We can discuss the reward if we find your dogs."

Christina sees her father looking in her direction. "Bye," she whispers, and quickly turns away.

Tina jerks her arm away from Randy and marches you toward the exit. Once you're out of earshot of the girls, Randy apologizes to Tina for not letting her take the money.

She laughs. "That's okay. I just wanted to call her bluff. She *expected* us to turn down the money. Little sneak."

You go outside to find Jack playing with Mara on the grass in front of City Hall. They're rolling on the ground, Mara gnarling and Jack laughing. She's got him pinned. After a few play-nips, she starts to lick his face.

"What a cute couple!" Tina says gleefully.

At the sound of her voice, Jack scrambles to his feet and tries to regain his dignity. "How was the hearing?"

You tell him what chaos it was. He nods sagely. "I've been studying this for the past couple of days. It's quite clear to me now. Human behavior is far more uncouth than dog behavior."

"We'll get to see plenty of both tomorrow," Tina says. "The Digital Detectives are going to the dog show!"

7

THE FANCY

The Digital Detectives meet at your house before the county dog show. All five of you gather in your room: Tina, Randy, Jack, Mara, and you. Normally Jack would be the one to try to organize everyone's thoughts on the case. But he's occupied. When he's not keeping Mara from jumping up on everything in your room, he's rubbing noses with her.

Tina has ceased to find it cute. She stands over him with her hands on her hips. "Are you going to play kissy-face all day, or are you going to help solve this crime?" she demands.

Jack just laughs. So instead, you take charge. Sitting at your computer, you decide to make a list of everything you know about the case, plus a list of what you want to check out during what Tina calls your "assault" on the dog show. She's been practicing tricks on her skateboard this morning and apparently is still in a Road Warrior frame of mind. She certainly looks the part, in her ripped jeans and elbow pads. Her hair is braided with leather thongs. You have to watch out for them when she turns her head.

"Item one," you begin, "missing dogs. Joe, of course. Christina's dog Redley. Lindsay's dog. And lots of others. Have they been stolen? Or are they lost? Or did they run away?"

"Or a combination of all three," Randy muses. "At the

show, we need to talk to everyone we can find who's lost a dog. Get descriptions. Learn how it happened. Look for the pattern."

"Right," you say, typing. "Second, Canigen Labs and Peter Frost. We need to find out more about them."

"We can ask people at the show," Tina says, "but probably we'll have to go to the lab ourselves. If they'll let us in."

"Third, the breeders," you go on. "Especially Crossley and Houston Smith. It sounds like there's a major feud there. Bad enough to cause some dog stealing, maybe. We should be able to learn more at the show."

"Yep," Randy agrees. "And TheDogBytes.com. I don't know what's going on there, but it's not very human-friendly. Did you notice at the hearing how Dooley said dogs might really be doing it?"

"Yeah, yeah, I'm looking into the web site," Jack murmurs from his position on the floor, tickling Mara's ears.

"There's also Elly Shotte," Tina puts in. "Anyone who hates dogs that much should be investigated."

"All right," you agree. "Plus, Molly and Mark. Maybe any-one who *loves* dogs that much should be investigated, too."

"They haven't done anything wrong," Tina asserts. "But sure, we can talk to them. They know a lot."

"I think that's enough," Randy concludes. "We've got plen-ty to investigate. The dog show is about to open."

Tina claps her hands at the two figures on the floor. "Let's roll." Jack turns over on his stomach and heaves himself to his feet. "Come on, doggie, doggie," Tina says. "Yes, poochie! And Mara, you can come, too."

Mara looks disappointed that the game is over. "I know, girl," Jack says to her. "But what can we do? They're the alpha dogs. We have to obey."

Then he says to the rest of you, "Do you know why dogs and people get along so well? It's because dogs assume we're part of their pack. And because we're usually larger, and we control the food, they assume we're the dominant members of the pack. So they defer to us. Most of the time."

He pats Mara again. "That's also why dogs bite little kids sometimes," he continues. "Since they're smaller, dogs think children should act submissive, like a puppy. If they don't, a dog will give them a disciplinary bite."

"So Jack," Tina says, "if you don't behave at this show, that means I can give you a disciplinary bite?"

Jack leans down to whisper a secret to Mara—except he makes sure you all can hear him. "You know who the top alpha dog is?" He points at Tina. "It's her, the red one! Shh, I know. I don't know how she got that position either."

Tina wheels around in an instant and snaps her fingers in Jack's face. "Heel!" she commands.

Jack's face drops, and he silently follows the rest of you out.

* * *

People are streaming into the fairgrounds. A giant white tent with twin peaks has been set up. The dog show is inside. But before you get to the entrance, Tina pulls you over to a guy who's handing out flyers.

He's wearing a baseball cap that reads *A.R.F.* "Boycott the show!" he cries. "Breeders are slavemasters!"

You grab one of the flyers. It's from the Animal Rights Force. Besides explaining why they don't like breeders, it also lists the other demands Molly made last night at the hearing.

"So you're with ARF," Tina says to him. "Do you know Molly and Mark?"

His face brightens. "Yeah, they're new members. They're great. Molly really, really loves animals. She'd do anything for them. I think she and Mark are inside." He smiles broadly. "Causing trouble, no doubt."

Randy and Jack are at the door already, so you move Tina along. You pay admission, and join the stream of dogs and dog lovers who've come to see the show. Randy has a picture of Joe. He stops everyone he can to ask if they've seen him.

"Sure, there are plenty of spaniel fanciers," a woman tells him. A ribbon on her lapel reads JUDGE. "Just keep going in this direction. That's where the dogs to be shown are kept in their dens. You'll find a whole section of cockers."

Randy thanks her. "I'm going over there," he tells you. "I'm sure nobody would bring Joe, but . . . I just have to look."

"We'll catch you later," Tina agrees.

You come to a canvas wall that creates another tent within the tent. When you poke your noses inside, you find that it's where the dogs are being shown. A ring has been set up. Folding chairs on a series of risers encircle the ring. You search for some empty seats. There are a few around a big man in blue. As you draw closer, you realize it's Dooley. You don't really want to sit with him, but on the other hand you might learn something. You compromise and lead Jack and Tina to seats behind and to the left of Dooley. He just stares straight ahead.

The first event begins. It's called Conformation. A set of dogs and trainers waits inside the ring. As each one's name is called, the trainer trots the dog around the ring for the judges to see. You're impressed by how precise the bearing and posture of the dogs are. They prance in step with the trainers' stride.

"What's Conformation?" Tina whispers.

"From the word conform," a rough voice answers. It's Dooley. As he turns, you see that he's wearing a pair of clean overalls. His hair is plastered neatly against his large, uneven skull. "The dogs are judged on whether they conform to the standard the club has set. Size, shape, ear length, and so on. They spend hours getting bathed and trimmed. They're hardly dogs any more."

"No kidding," Tina agrees.

"Conformation," Dooley repeats. "Perfect word, eh? Make dogs conform to a fancy idea of what they should be. Did you know that's what they call this whole thing? 'The fancy.' And they call themselves dog 'fanciers.' Figures, huh?"

"So why are you here, Dooley?" you venture.

He gives you a long glance. "Why not? It's my day off. Got to do something."

"So you're not here to—" Jack begins.

"It's my day off," he repeats firmly. His eyes fall to Mara. "How's she working out?"

Tina rolls her eyes. "They're in love."

For the first time, you see Dooley smile. He holds out his hand and Mara comes eagerly to lick it. He seems to know all the right places to pet her. "Ahh, I'm glad you got a good home, girl. I'll tell Hotbreath. He'll be happy."

Someone turns around to shush him. But before you can stop yourself, you repeat, "Hotbreath."

Dooley gives you a glance. Hotbreath was another dog on the web site. Could Dooley be the one behind it? It seems he's almost trying to hint to you that he is.

You watch another round of the competition. Dooley grabs a bag of food from under his seat and begins to gnaw on a drumstick. Tina lets out a bored sigh. "Next?

"We're not learning much here," you agree. Only Jack and Mara seem interested. "We're going to look around," you tell them. Jack nods and says he'll be along in a little while.

"Dooley's not so bad," Tina comments as you reach the exit from the show tent. "Definitely weird, but not so bad."

"He might be the one behind the web site," you announce. Tina gapes at you. "He just mentioned the name of a dog on TheDogBytes.com," you explain.

"That doesn't mean he's doing it," Tina points out. "He could just be reading it. Or posting messages."

"Maybe he's not the secret dog-meister," you admit. "But he was letting me in on a secret. I could tell."

"Secret dog-meister?" a voice demands.

You stop abruptly as you practically run into Molly and Mark. She spreads her arms and gives Tina a big smile. "What brings *you* here?"

Tina smiles back. "Looking around. But I didn't expect to see *you*. What are you doing here?"

Molly shifts her eyes mischievously from right to left. "Oh, you know. Subversion. Sabotage. The usual. So now tell me—what's this about a secret dog-meister?"

"Oh, we were just talking about TheDogBytes.com," Tina explains. "We think we know who's behind it."

Mark's brows arch. "Who would that be?"

"It's—" Tina jerks as you give her a hidden pinch. "Well, we're not sure yet, to tell the truth."

Molly looks at Mark, then leans over to squeeze Tina's elbow confidentially. "I don't think *anyone's* behind it.

Anyone human, that is. Of course, some of us might be helping the dogs out just a little bit."

"You mean—" But before Tina can go on, the look on Molly's face turns to horror. She stares at her hand, which has moved to grasp one of the leather thongs in Tina's hair.

"Tina!" Molly shrieks. "You're wearing leather! This is criminal!" Molly tries to rip the thong out of her hair. "Take it off!"

"Hey," Tina objects. "You're hurting me!"

Tina wrenches Molly's arm away. Molly has a wild look in her eyes. Mark reaches for Molly, but with one hand holding a backpack strap, he can't quite stop her. "Take it easy, Molly."

Tina backs away slowly. You're right beside her. "How could you?" Molly shrieks. She knocks Mark's arm aside, but at that moment another figure steps in front of her. It's Peter Frost.

"Leave that girl alone," he orders, drawing himself up.

Molly stops and glares at him. By now other people are watching. Holding his briefcase in front of him as a kind of shield, Peter goes on the attack. "You're the one who splashed blood all over my auto, aren't you?" he demands. "You have no respect for human beings, only animals. And here I thought you were one of the reasonable ones. You ruined my car!"

"You deserve worse," Molly declares fiercely.

You and Tina get away as fast as you can. "Are you all right?" you ask.

"I'm fine," Tina says, still steamed. "How dare she!"

"She just totally bugged."

"It's like she turned into some kind of animal." Tina lets

out a little laugh. "Which I guess to her isn't an insult."

"Maybe Peter Frost is right. Maybe she loves animals but hates people."

Tina just shakes her head. You can tell she's spitting mad at Molly, but at the same time her feelings are hurt. "I can't believe she did that to you!" you say. "I hope she didn't ruin your braids—"

But Tina cuts you off. "Never mind. Let's go find Randy."

✳ ✳ ✳

You and Tina walk on over to the benching area where the dogs are kept. It's a large open space under the big tent, filled with rows and rows of pens for the dogs.

It takes a while to figure out where to look for Randy. The pens are organized by seven dog types: Sporting, Working, Hound, Herding, Terrier, Toy, and Non-Sporting. You notice that some of the pens have yellow ribbons on them. These pens are empty. A notice on one says, "My name is Biscuit. I wish I was here. If you've seen me, please contact my owner." The owner's name and number are given, alongside a picture of Biscuit.

"The yellow ribbons must be for the missing dogs," Tina notes. You look down the row together. It's dotted with yellow. The sight makes you sad. All those dogs—where are they?

A pair of well-dressed girls emerges from the crowd. They see you and give a wave. It's Christina and Lindsay. Each carries a stylish little purse. Christina flashes her perfect white teeth. "Did you see the yellow ribbons?"

"That was our idea. We've started a web registry, too,"

Lindsay says. "We're creating an on-line support community. You can register the name and breed of your missing dog."

"Wait a minute," Tina objects. "It's only for purebreds?"

Christina and Lindsay look at each other as if it hadn't occurred to them that other kinds of dogs exist. "Um, no, it's for anyone, I guess," Lindsay says. "It just seems like it's mostly purebreds that have been taken."

"Maybe you need to widen your social circle," Tina observes.

"Where's your dad?" you ask Christina. "He must be here."

"Oh yes. And he's letting me use one of his dogs for the junior competition, since Redley is missing. Come on, I'll show you our pens."

Lindsay splits off to find her own parents. You and Tina follow Christina through the benching area. As you walk, you summon up the courage to ask Christina a question. "So what's the problem between your dad and Houston Smith?"

She frowns. "Houston is just a . . . well, it's ridiculous. My dad had a litter that looks, I guess, like one of Houston's prize hounds. The hound was missing for a little while, so Houston thought my dad stole him in order to breed him. But I happen to know my dad worked very hard with a gene specialist to produce the litter."

"You mean he created it in a petri dish or something?" Tina says.

"No, they implanted—well, I'm not supposed to talk about it. I'm sorry." She waves, and you see her father across the way. He's standing by a table in front of his pens. On the table is information about his breeds.

"Here we are," Christina says. "You can see them for your-selves. We brought a number of our prize dogs. Some are for show, some for breeding, and some for sale. If you're interested."

Mr. Crossley gives you and Tina a quick nod in greeting, then barks an order to Christina. "You need to clean up Elroy's cage. I can't handle it all myself."

"Yes, Daddy." She gives you an apologetic look, then grabs a little hand shovel and bag. You can't keep from watching as she wades into one of the straw-floored cages in her new shoes. But Tina is gazing up the aisle. She tugs on your sleeve. You look over to see Houston Smith strolling in your direction, along with Darwina Lopez and another woman who is quite tall.

"Daddy," Christina calls, "I think Elroy's upset. He really misses Redley. He's not happy at all."

"Now, Christina," Crossley calls back. "I've told you a thousand times, dogs don't have emotions. Not like we do."

By now Darwina is within earshot. "Of course they have emotions, Bertram," she says to Crossley. "Darwin himself wrote a paper on the subject. Who do you think I was named after?"

Crossley looks up. The thin smile meant for Darwina flattens into displeasure when he sees Houston.

But Houston's expression is quite different. He's gripping a tall cup with something frothy inside. His face is a bit red. He appears to be enjoying himself, and Crossley's displeasure increases his good mood. "If it isn't good ol' Bertram! Getting ready for the competition? Better keep an eye on your dogs, son. Oh, but don't worry while you're in the ring. We'll tend them for you."

"As if you haven't already made a big enough fool of yourself at the hearing," Crossley mutters. Then he puts a smile back on for Darwina and says, "I guess we'll just have to agree to disagree on the question of emotions. I still respect your medical talents, as you know."

"Thank you," Darwina says dryly. "Bertram, did you ever meet Patty? She's quite a fancier, as you people would say."

Darwina's friend Patty has to bend slightly to shake Crossley's hand. Then she holds out a hand to you and Tina as well. You've never met a woman with a crew cut before, but it looks pretty good on her. Her earrings are in the shape of two large dog bones.

The polite smiles fade as the assembled group realizes they have nothing to say to each other. You feel like this is your big chance to ask some questions, so you desperately try to think of one. But you're interrupted by a shriek, then a yowl.

A cat comes streaking down the aisle. It's followed by a shrieking Elly Shotte. She's got another cat cradled against her shoulder. In a single motion, Patty swoops down and picks up the fleeing cat. Holding it under its stomach, she lifts it high in the air so that it can't claw her.

"Elly!" Houston barks. "What are you doing with—"

But he's interrupted too, by a sudden onslaught of dogs. They come charging down the aisle, their eyes fixed on the cat. You and Tina are banged against one of the cages and knocked off your feet. Patty is knocked down as well. She loses her grip on the cat. It seems to jump about five feet in the air, somehow hovering above the mass of barking dogs, its fur standing on end as if it's just been plugged into a wall socket.

"What's going on here?" Crossley shouts.

By some miracle the cat dashes away. The dogs chase after it. But the chaos doesn't end there. More dogs have gotten out of their pens. They're thundering in from every direction. The hall has become a writhing mass of fur and tails, and caught in the middle are stumbling owners trying to catch them. You and Tina huddle against the cage, making yourselves as small as you can. Somewhere you hear the screech of Elly's cat, then the screeching of Elly herself.

Darwina is standing atop Crossley's table. From her vantage point, she calls out, "Someone's opened the pens!"

The place is in full-fledged panic. Dogs are everywhere, running, barking, panting, and generally having a good time. Houston Smith is laughing uproariously, the front of his shirt covered with beer. The dogs all seem to be running in one general direction. Houston goes after them.

"Someone opened the exits!" Darwina cries.

Dogs stream out of the tent, chased by their owners. Darwina, Patty, and Crossley follow, but you and Tina stay curled up where you are. For a while all you see from your spot on the ground, pressed up against an empty cage, is a stampede of feet and paws.

Then, all of a sudden, it is quiet again. Tina taps you on the shoulder. "I think it's safe to stand up."

You brush yourself off and take in the scene before you. Most of the cages that you can see have been opened. A few are still locked, with the dogs inside their pens. They whine forlornly after their pals. Straw, blankets, papers, and personal effects are strewn across the floors. Otherwise the tent is eerily quiet. The hunt has gone outdoors.

"This is our chance," Tina announces. "Get out the JackPack. Let's see if we can dig up some evidence on these people."

"Right," you say, as the brilliance of her idea dawns on you. This is a perfect opportunity to snoop, especially if people have left behind their stuff in the rush to catch the dogs.

Start snooping around on
the Digital Detectives web site:

http://www.ddmysteries.com
and enter the key phrase **DOGSHOW**

When you've finished the investigation, the web site will give you a page number to return to.

8

PUPPY LOVE

"Joe!" you exclaim.

"Yes, it's Joe!" Tina cries with you.

Jack rubs Mara behind the ears. "It was Mara who found him. I knew she had a good nose. I asked Randy to lend me couple of Joe's things, so she could get to know his scent. And here he is!"

Joe wags his tail madly and licks your hand through the cage. The only problem is, he's still locked inside. His wasn't one of the cages opened. You notice that the owner of this cage and the one next to it—which is open and empty—is named Suzy Lindman. "Suzy's going to have a lot of questions to answer when she gets back," you say.

People are starting to filter back into the tent now. The chase seems to be over. There's a general buzz as everyone tries to figure out how the dogs got loose. The two wire clippers you found during your investigation will help explain it. But you still have to figure out who used them. And why.

Tina decides she's going to go find Randy and tell him about Joe. You sit in a chair next to Joe's cage and let him lick your hand while you wait.

A few minutes later a woman with bobbed blond hair and a beaming expression on her face comes around the corner. She has a big rottweiler on a leash. The minute it sees you it tries to come after you. The woman pulls with all her might to restrain the growling dog.

"Missy!" she commands. "Down!"

You, Jack, and Mara crowd together for protection. That is one large and determined dog, you think. Missy barks insanely. "Um, maybe you should move away from the cage," the woman suggests.

As soon as you do, Missy's expression changes. Her eyes go all soft. Her tail wags. What's even more amazing is that Joe is doing exactly the same thing. The two dogs meet and exchange nuzzles and licks through the grille of the cage.

"Sorry," the woman says, "but no one can keep them apart."

"You must be Suzy," you reply. When she nods, you point at Joe. "That dog belongs to a friend of ours."

Suzy's eyes widen. "Really? Oh, I'm so glad you found him. He didn't have any tags, and I just didn't know what to do with him!"

You regard her twinkling eyes for a moment. She seems to be speaking honestly. "Yeah, well . . . how'd you get him, anyway?"

"He followed us home! Well, not me, but Missy. We were at Portola Grove. I could see they were getting along pretty well. He must have snuck into my car while we were leaving. Next thing I knew, there he was at my house. He and Missy could not bear to be separated. They're like Romeo and Juliet."

"But didn't you see our posters?" Jack wonders. "Or our notices on the Internet?"

Suzy squints. "No . . . I've been meaning to go back to Portola Grove, but I haven't had time yet. And I don't have e-mail."

Jack's jaw drops. He gapes at her. "Are you Amish?"

Suzy laughs. "No, silly! I just don't have it. I design curtains. What do I need the Internet for?"

Jack continues to stare at Suzy. He's still processing this information when you hear a roar from down the aisle. "JOE!!!"

It's Randy. He dashes to the cage and tries to push his arms through to hug Joe. Joe jumps up and down to greet him. To your surprise, Missy just stands aside. Maybe she can see how much Randy means to Joe.

Suzy opens the cage so that Randy can take Joe up into his arms. You and she repeat the whole story for him. Randy nods and grins the whole time, while Joe licks his face. Tina's right next to him, scratching Joe's back.

"This is exactly why I brought him here," Suzy beams. "I hoped his owner would come! And, voila!"

"Thank you," Randy keeps saying. "Can I give you a reward?"

Suzy won't hear of it. She's just relieved that he and Joe have been reunited. She apologizes for not finding Randy sooner. "I guess Missy will have to say good-bye to him," she concludes, wiping away a mock tear. "Maybe he can come over to visit."

"For sure," Randy agrees. "Thank you for bringing him. Thank you for taking such good care of him."

Suzy waves as the six of you begin to leave. Missy cocks her head. A melancholy expression comes over her, such as you never could have imagined on a rottweiler's face. Joe looks back sadly, too. Then he looks at Randy, then back at Missy. He seems torn. But once you get him out of sight of Missy, his attention turns to Randy and their happy reunion.

✳ ✳ ✳

Once you get back to Randy's house, you have a chance to compare notes on the dog show. You go out to his back patio, lemonade in hand. The weather is still fair. It's a perfect afternoon to sit outside. Mara and Joe play on the grass.

First, you and Tina give a short rundown of what you found in your investigation while everyone was out of the tent. "It was a perfect setup," Tina exults. "Everybody left their stuff behind and we got to poke through it."

"I guess we can thank whoever was using those wire clippers to cut open the cages," you say. "If we can identify the prints on the clippers, we'll know who was behind that."

"Yes, but don't make any leaps of logic," Jack corrects. "That could be a very different thing than whoever is taking the dogs."

"True," you agree. "We need to figure out a motive. That'd help us know better what we're looking for."

"Yep, a motive. And the means. And the opportunity," Tina says, ticking off the three elements behind every crime.

"Okay, possible motives," Randy theorizes. "One, to take revenge. Maybe it's a rivalry between breeders, like Crossley and Smith. Or it's Elly Shotte, because she hates dogs."

"All three have strong motives," you agree.

"Two," Randy goes on, "to make money. Maybe by selling the dogs or using them to breed prize dogs. Or for research, like at Canigen Labs."

"We've got to check out Canigen," Tina states. "Everybody's got a connection to them. ARF hates them. Crossley's doing some kind of business with them. So are Norris and Darwina."

"Three," Randy goes on. "Dog, uh, liberation."

"You mean like on TheDogBytes?" you put in. "All those dogs talking about leaving behind humans and escaping to Dog Wood? Molly did act like she was part of it."

"Exactly. That's the kind of motive that would come from ARF."

"Molly is definitely kind of rabid," Tina declares. She tells Randy about their run-in. "I mean, I thought she was a pretty cool person. But pulling my hair, that was not cool."

"There's Dooley, too," you observe. "He also dropped a hint that he's in on TheDogBytes.com."

"If there's one person who's got the means to collect a lot of dogs, it's Dooley," Tina points out.

"And the opportunity. We don't know where he was when all those dogs at the show got out," you agree. "We don't know where Molly and Mark were either. All three dislike breeders, which could be a motive. We do know that Houston, Darwina, and Crossley were with us."

"That doesn't mean anything," Tina objects. "People like those breeders would have some lackey do the dirty work."

"Right," Jack says. He taps the side of his face, thinking. "Now, am I wrong, or is it mostly purebreds that have gone missing?"

The three of you nod. "It does seem that way," Randy says. "Everyone I talked to lost a purebred. Of course, Joe's not, though people might mistake him for one."

"But Joe's disappearance was an exception," you remind him. "It was just an accident that he fell in love with Missy. Unless—all the rest are accidents, too."

Everyone groans. This idea makes the case seem hopeless. What if each dog is missing for a different reason?

"All right, forget I said that," you say. "We've got plenty of things to investigate. We need to keep looking for patterns. Like the fact that some dogs are going hungry. How come that's happening? And is it related to the missing purebreds?"

After mystified shrugs all around, Tina comes up with a plan of action. "There are a lot of things to check out. We need to split up the work, like before. We'll each write a report on what we find out. Then we'll read them tomorrow night and decide what to do."

The three of you quickly agree. You begin choosing who each of you will interview. Tina doesn't want to talk to Molly, so Jack volunteers to take on ARF. He also wants to talk to Dooley for himself, and promises to see if he can uncover more information about the TheDogBytes.com.

Tina decides she'll invade the Highlands Kennel Club and try to find the Crossleys and Houston Smith. Randy offers to look up Darwina Lopez, Mr. Norris, and Mr. Kuo.

"Wait a minute," you object. "That leaves me with Peter Frost and Canigen Labs. The hardest one."

"And Elly Shotte," Tina puts in. "But if you're not up to it, just say so."

Tina has a way of getting you to do things you would never normally think of trying. In the past, you've always ended up feeling pretty brave. So you decide to take the challenge again.

"Don't worry," you answer. "I'm up for it."

✳ ✳ ✳

You get home in time for dinner, even more exhausted than the day before. You're so hungry that you wolf down two portions of dinner. Your mom reminds you to eat like a person, not a wild beast. "Maybe I've been spending too much time around dogs," you murmur.

Your family congratulates you on your success in finding Joe at the dog show. But you tell them the case is not closed. There are many dogs still missing. There may be a dognapper at work. "I guess that means you'll keep investigating," your mom sighs.

"Yeah, we're doing some things tomorrow. If that's all right," you respond.

Your parents look at each other and then nod. By now you've had enough success as a detective that they're willing to cut you some slack. "Just be safe," your dad says.

After dinner, you get to thinking about animal rights. You log on do some research on the subject. The theory of animal rights is based on the idea that animals are conscious, feeling beings very similar to humans. The people who oppose this view say that there's a key difference between humans and animals. Humans are "moral agents"—meaning they can make choices between right and wrong. Animals just do what they do by instinct.

You're not sure which side you're on. While dogs may lack the kind of verbal language humans have, they do seem to live by a social code. They often appear better at sticking to the code than humans. But it's also true that the code is based on which dog can assert dominance. Does this make them less ethical than people? Or is the code just programmed into their genes anyhow?

Then again, some scientists say human behavior is also mere genetic coding. Does the real difference between us boil down to the fact that each species only sees things from its own selfish point of view? If so, can it be said that one is really morally superior to the other? Since dogs can't talk, we can't really find out what's going on in their minds.

Your head spinning, you surf over to TheDogBytes.com to see what the dogs have to say. Now it dawns on you what this web site is all about. Unless someone really has found a way to channel telepathic dog thoughts into web postings—which is pretty dubious—it's an effort by certain humans to put themselves in the shoes of another species. Or in this case, the paws.

Sometimes it really works. Reading the messages makes you feel like you're getting a glimpse into another world. You never thought about the fact that maybe some dogs like to be with humans, and some don't. Maybe it's true that there are a lot of dogs who'd just as soon leave people behind and go live in Dog Wood—if it really exists.

Scrolling to the latest posts, you see that the dog show is a big topic. Some want to know who opened the cages. Some are eager to hear if anyone caught the cat that was loose. Others say that all shows ought to be this much fun. In response to them, dogs like Wolf8 and Red Ears say they should forget about shows and come live in Dog Wood, where it's fun all the time.

Then you find some messages from dogs who have done just that. Dogs named Snowball, Monty, Annabelle, and Spike write that the big melee allowed them to escape from the show and come to Dog Wood.

That makes you wonder. You look up the web site Christina has started. Several new names have been added to the list of missing dogs. They all disappeared yesterday at the dog show. You check the names—sure enough, Snowball,

Monty, Annabelle, and Spike are on it. All purebreds.

You also find a message from Christina. Its content surprises you.

> Many thanks to Dooley for helping us get our dogs back in their pens. He was absolutely heroic. Without his expert wrangling, many more dogs would have been lost.

You copy the message and forward it to the other Digital Detectives. Then you shut down your computer. It's time for some sleep.

You go to bed scratching your head. It seems more and more like Dog Wood might be a real place. You remember the map you found in the TheDogBytes clubhouse. There was an area marked DW. It now seems like a very good idea to investigate it. You decide you'll do so tomorrow, after your trip to Canigen Labs.

9
WET MEDICINE

It's about noon on Sunday when you set off on your mountain bike for Canigen Labs, butterflies in your stomach. You keep asking yourself, "What's the worst that can happen?" Luckily the answer you come up with is that Peter Frost refuses to answer your questions. At least, that's what you tell yourself.

The weather has changed a bit today. A new storm will arrive from the northwest sometime tomorrow. The winds have shifted. They blow chilly and cold off the Pacific. A march of clouds blocks out the sun.

Canigen is out near the small city airport. You turn off of Airport Road and follow a winding drive a little way into the hills to the east. The drive ends at a business park, a cluster of office buildings set among some trees and grass. Of course, you don't even know if you'll find Frost here on a Sunday. The place looks deserted as you turn into the parking lot.

You approach a long, low building with a snazzy Canigen logo on the front. The building looks expensive, with steel and granite facing. The front door is open, but right inside is a security guard. You tell him you'd like to see Peter Frost.

The guard looks you over, then picks up a phone. Shoot. You were half-hoping Frost wouldn't be here. Then you wouldn't have to ask the hard questions you have for him.

Peter Frost comes into the lobby a minute later. He's wearing a T-shirt, board shorts, and sandals. You remind him that you met when he helped out Tina during the little snarl with Molly at yesterday's dog show. His face brightens, as he assumes you're no friend of Molly. He invites you to his office.

You notice that his T-shirt has a surfboard on it. You ask if he's caught any waves lately. He sweeps his sun-streaked hair away from his face and leans back in his chair. "Yeh, there was a good swell last week," he says in his Aussie accent. "Just before that storm. You get it?"

You nod. Tina and Randy have been teaching you to surf. "Maybe there's another one coming with the next storm," you add. This is good, you think. You're both surfers. You have a bond.

"Good chance of it," he replies. "That's why I came in today, to get ahead on my work. Now, what can I do for you?"

You glance around his office. There are many pictures of dogs. They look like pages from a book. Each one shows an exemplary dog and lists the characteristics of its breed.

Taking a guess, you say, "You work with purebreds."

Peter nods. "Yes. We're trying to isolate a certain gene, which is much easier to do using a small, genetically homogeneous population. We use the purest of the pure."

"What's your research about?" you ask.

He flashes you a big-toothed smile. "I could tell you, but then I'd have to kill you."

You laugh nervously. You know he's joking, but still . . .

Frost's smile disappears. He makes a tent with his fingers. "This is a highly competitive field. I can't tell you details.

But the gene will allow us to diagnose a disease that makes certain dogs go blind. Then, I hope, we can find a way to cure the disease. So it's all for a good cause. That's what people like Molly don't seem to understand. They think we're torturing dogs. Well, we're not. We do need to keep them here so we can study them. But we treat them very well."

"Can I see them?"

Frost shakes his head. "I'm sorry, we don't let anyone back there without security clearance. I can't break my own company's rules. But we did take some dogs to the show. I don't know if you saw them."

You take a deep breath. Here comes the hard question. "Yes, we saw your pens. We also happened to, um, find out that you're doing business with Mr. Crossley."

Frost's eyes narrow. "So?"

"A lot of dogs are missing. All purebreds." You squirm a bit, unsure yourself what the connection might be. "We're trying to find out why."

"Ah. So *you* suspect me too." Frost drums his fingers on the desk. "I don't have to tell you this. But I want to put your fears to rest. I did help Crossley produce a litter of pups. There were some special genetic traits he wanted. In return, he has invested in the lab. It's all perfectly innocent."

"Would the Highlands Kennel Club see it that way?" you wonder. "It seems like it could mess up their whole system."

Suddenly Frost slaps his desk with a loud *thwap*, making you jump. He leans forward. His gray-blue eyes burn into you. "There is nothing illegal about our deal. I gave you this information in confidence. I expect you to keep it that way."

You shrink back in your chair. "I will."

Just then the phone rings. Frost picks it up and speaks for

a moment. As he talks, he swivels in his chair so that his back is turned. You sneak your digital camera out of your pack and snap a quick picture of the office.

"Yes. All right," he's saying. "That's too bad. We'll have to find another collie, then. Soon." Frost hangs up the phone, turns back to you, and attempts a smile. "Are we done?"

"Um, just one other thing. You also seem to have a connection to Mr. Norris at the pound. Is he an investor, too?"

Frost throws up his arms. "What a busybody! Why can't you be like other kids and—" He stops abruptly and looks out the window. "All right. This is also confidential, only because certain people might get even more hostile to us if they knew. We do occasionally take dogs from the pound. You have to understand that purebreds are very hard to find. Every once in a while the pound gets one that meets our needs. Rather than let the dog go without a home, we take it in here. That's all."

"Oh. Well, that seems like a good idea," you say uncertainly. "What do you do when you're done with them?"

Frost's lips compress and he locks in on you with his gaze. "They stay with us for the length of their natural lives."

"Okay." You don't dare pursue the question further. Already you feel intimidated—both by his intensity and by the fact he's confided so much information to you.

Frost leans forward again. "If you're trying to find the dogs," he says in a low voice, "I'll tell you who to look at very closely. It's that Molly, from the Animal Rights Force. Some of those people are reasonable, but some aren't. She's not. She'll stop at nothing. She probably thinks she's saving the dogs somehow. You saw her in action for yourself at the show yesterday."

96

You nod. "Thanks for the tip. And thanks for talking to me."

"My pleasure." Frost walks you back to the lobby. "Good luck," he says, nearly crushing your hand in his suntanned grip.

You unlock your bike, feeling pretty good about the interview, except when you flex your injured fingers. At least he took you seriously. That doesn't always happen with adults. In fact, you're amazed at how much he was willing to tell you.

The question is, is it because he really wants to help? Or is it because he has so much to hide?

* * *

You start to ride out of the parking lot. You need to visit Elly Shotte next. But an opening in the trees just beyond the outer edge of the parking lot catches your eye. It's the entrance to a fire trail. A fire trail is a kind of jeep road maintained by the county. There's a whole system of them in the hills above Crescent Bay. They make for great mountain bike riding.

You picture the town's geography in your mind. To get to Elly's house you'd have to go downhill to Airport Road and then climb back up into the Portola Grove neighborhood. But this fire trail might take you on a more direct route up and across the ridge above town, allowing you to drop down to Elly's house from above. Plus, from what you remember of the map in the clubhouse, Dog Wood might be right in the area you'd come down through to get to Portola Grove.

Might as well try it, you think. You've got your bike helmet.

You pedal across the lot, jump the curb, and start up the dirt trail. It's a bit rough from winter storms, but rideable.

Soon you have to gear down as the climb up the ridge begins. After a while, the eucalyptus turns to laurel and oak. A couple of riders pass going the other way. They wave cheerfully.

You've worked up a good sweat by the time you reach the ridge crest. From up here, you can see neat lines of waves corrugating the ocean water. Peter Frost was right. The surfing will be good.

A pair of riders pauses nearby to take in the view. You ask them if there's a trail that drops down into Portola Grove.

"Yep," one of them says. "Just take your second right."

Perfect. You push off and pedal along the crest of the ridge. The chill wind is still blowing, but the uphill climb has warmed you. You feel great.

You pass one turnoff, then point your wheels downhill when you come to the second. Ahh, now comes the easy part. You're cruising down, coming around a bend, when suddenly you have to slam on your brakes to avoid two hikers. As you veer out of their way, you are startled for a moment when you think it's Mark and Molly. You start to wave, then as you pass realize it's not them.

The man glares at you. "Slow down!" he barks.

You decide that's a good idea. You're getting close to the area where Dog Wood might be. You need to keep your eyes peeled.

It's a good thing, because you probably would have missed the trail going off into the woods on your left. It's a fairly large trail, four or five feet wide, but both the ground and the woods are dark. It could easily be passed by.

You skid to a stop and pedal over to the trail. Taking a breath, you start down it. It plunges into a broad hollow, dense with trees. You've got your hands on your brakes the whole time.

The trail comes to a rushing creek, and you have to make a quick decision. You plunge into the creek on your bike. That turns out to be the wrong choice. After hitting a couple of rocks, you come churning to a stop. You have to put your feet down in the cold water and walk your bike the rest of the way across. Your shoes are soaked.

The trail climbs a bit on the other side of the creek. You pedal slowly. You think you hear a bark from somewhere below, and stop to listen. Yes, there's another bark. But you also hear footsteps pounding behind you. Before you can turn, something goes whizzing by your ear. A stone!

A quick glance back gives you only a brief look at a male figure. Yikes! His eyes are hidden behind dark glasses, a hat is pulled low over his forehead and the rest of his face is masked by a dark bandanna. He hurls another stone at you.

You jump back on your bike and pedal for all you're worth. The trail flattens, then starts downhill again. Good. You'll be able to outdistance your pursuer on your bike.

You race along, struggling to fight down the fear rising in your throat. But soon you have to slam on your brakes again. A big tree trunk is blocking the trail. You have no time to come to a full stop. You jerk up desperately on the handlebars of your bike to half-jump, half-bump over the trunk. Thank goodness you make it, you think, or you'd be at the mercy of your pursuer.

No sooner has your vision cleared than another obstacle appears. It looks like some kind of home-made camp. You get a fast glimpse of a wooden shelf built between two trees, some burlap sacks, and—

What's this in the middle of the forest? A barbed-wire fence! Right in front of you! This time you're out of luck. Your bike slams into the wire fence and stays there. You go sailing off the seat, head over heels. It all happens in incredibly slow motion. The world turns upside down, then suddenly, with a painful jolt to your backside, comes right side up again.

You feel your arms and legs. You're all in one piece. You look up. The masked figure is leaping over the tree trunk. You have no choice. You'll have to shake off your daze, right now, and abandon the bike. It's still tangled in the barbed wire.

You jump to your feet and, leaving the trail behind, race down through the wood. Branches slash at your face as you dodge between the trees, around boulders, and over fallen trunks. You don't care. You just concentrate on cutting a narrow path through the woods as you try to keep yourself from crying out in fear.

Then suddenly you realize someone is racing along with you. But it's not your pursuer. It's a dog, an Irish setter. Christina's dog Redley! He appears to be grinning at you. Does he think it's some kind of game? Or maybe he just recognizes you from a few days ago.

You have no time to find out. You just keep running, desperately trying to put distance between you and whoever is chasing you. But out of the corner of your eye, you realize Redley is not the only dog here. There are others. A husky. A border terrier. A corgi. A French spaniel with red ears. Some of them give a bark as you go by, some just watch. You've found Dog Wood!

There's no time to investigate now. All you want to do is escape. After a few more heart-pounding minutes, you come to another fence. It's closely strung barbed wire, just like the first one. The strands are too dense for you to squeeze through. But you find a tree nearby. You're able to climb it, crawl along a branch, and drop down on the other side of the fence.

You can't stop running yet. You're soon on your feet again. At last you see light ahead. Just when you think your lungs are about to burst, you come crashing out of the woods and roll to a stop on some nice soft grass.

Several dogs come to sniff you. But when they smell your blood, their manner changes. Knowing you're injured, they step back respectfully.

Now a face you recognize is standing over you. It's one of the dog walkers from Portola Grove. That must be where you are.

"Are you all right?" the man asks.

You sit up and take stock. Your face is scraped and bruised. Your shirt is torn. Fine threads of blood well up from the scratches on your arms. But you're intact. And actually, you feel okay. Considering.

You can't quite think how to explain this to the man, so you just say, "I had a bike accident."

He pulls out a cell phone. "Can I call someone for you?"

You give him your home number. Luckily your dad is there. He promises to come right over to pick you up.

You thank the man for his help. He wants to stay until your dad arrives, but you assure him, "I'll be fine. Thank you for helping."

"You're welcome," he replies, and moves a few feet away, still keeping an eye on you.

You lay back to rest for just a minute. One of the dogs gives a little whine and comes over to check on you. The next thing you know, a warm tongue is licking at the scrapes on your cheek. It stings, but at the same time it feels good. You just close your eyes and let the wet medicine do its work.

10
THE REPORTS

Once you get yourself cleaned up, you don't look so bad. The scratches make crisscross patterns on your arms and face. There's a bruise on your cheek that's going to turn nice and purple over the next few days. It should impress your friends.

All you tell your parents is that you took a spill while riding down the ridge. You leave out the part about being chased. They give you a lecture about being careful on your bike and the importance of wearing your helmet at all times. You've already thanked yourself many times for having it on when the crash occurred. They ask if you want them to drive you back up to retrieve your bike. You say it can wait until tomorrow.

When you feel like yourself again, you call the others. Jack is the only one home. You tell him about your accident, and about finding Dog Wood. "I don't know if all the dogs are there," you say. "But Redley was, and a few others. Should we call the police?"

"Hmm," Jack ponders. "Let's not, just yet. Let's do a little more investigation and see if we can give them the perpetrator too. If there's a fence around the wood, the dogs aren't going anywhere."

"Okay," you agree. "We can all read each other's reports

tonight. There's one more thing I want to know now—where was each of the suspects around three o'clock, when I was chased?"

"We'll check into that," Jack says. "Just take it easy for the rest of the day."

What's left of the afternoon is spent playing with your sister Eve. She's disturbed by the condition of your face, and you figure it'll make her feel better if you act normal. Come to think of it, it makes you feel better, too.

Your dad cooks the Sunday usual for dinner, hamburgers on the charcoal grill. Once dinner is over, you feel ready to face your computer and write up your report. By the time you're done, the reports from the others have come in. You print them and settle down to read.

TINA'S REPORT

I put the Highlands Kennel Club in my crosshairs for about noon, figuring they'll all want to get together and talk about the wonderful dog show. Right as usual. Not that the likes of me'd ever get past the gate, but I lie and tell them I'm a friend of Christina and Lindsay. Luckily they're both right there under a pink umbrella on the patio. These fine young ladies help out by acting like I actually am their friend, so the guy at the gate can stop giving me the fishy eyeball. We chat. They're all, "Isn't this doggie cute, isn't that one fine," and so on. I say to Christina she doesn't seem very upset about the missing Redley. She assured me she's *very* distraught. I don't know, maybe these people just keep their emotions shut up in jars.

Anyway, I start trying to pry the lid off. I ask what's going on between her dad and Peter Frost. She tries to wiggle out of it. She started to spill the beans to us at the dog show, so I say don't try to pretend. How can we get her dog back for her if she doesn't fully cooperate? Finally she coughs up that Canigen helped them breed a litter that, as it turns out, bore no small resemblance to Houston Smith's prize hound. She wants to make sure I understand that no dog was stolen or anything.

Then she gets this devilish little look on her face and for a minute I actually like her. "One little hair from Houston's hound," she says. "That's all it took. One hair!"

Well, this here club is a small world, so it doesn't take long for someone who overhears to tell someone who tells someone and pretty soon Houston himself is standing in front of us, swelling up like a big red balloon. When the hot air comes out, it goes something like this: "I knew it. Your father ripped me off. He stole my dog's DNA. I'm going to sic the police on him."

(Sorry, I'm omitting the colorful language he actually used.)

Christina acts like she knows for a fact that borrowing a little DNA (if that's what happened) isn't a crime. Maybe she's even right. But Lindsay tugs her arm and whispers in her ear. Christina's mouth turns into a little "o" when she realizes she just let it slip to Houston that her father did it.

Houston starts bellowing, "Where is he? Where's your father?" like he's going to challenge him to a duel, until another gentleman suggests it's improper to yell at two such well-bred young ladies. (Notice he says *two*.)

Now, I actually do need to know where Crossley is. He's not here, of course. He avoids the club these days because of Houston. I finally get from Christina that he's playing golf. Great. I'm going to have to track him down on the links. I'm just bouncing from one great party to the next.

First, though, I stop inside at the bar to find out if Houston has anything else to say. He must know I'm a detective now, because he wants to hire me to nail Crossley. I assure him the truth will come out. (That's what we're supposed to say, right?)

When I bring up the dog show, he cheers up. "Everyone's playing the blame game today, trying to figure whose fault it was.

I say it's just what the show needed. Who cares if half of the competitions got cancelled? That was a riot!"

"Plus, Mr. Crossley didn't get to show his new and improved crop of dogs," I suggest.

Smith just smirks, orders himself a drink, and says I'm too smart for my own good. I take in the crowd for a minute, which is enough to decide me on leaving. People are starting to look at me like I don't belong, or if I do I should be back in the kitchen washing dishes.

I roll down to Bill Cabot's (remember him?) country club, where Crossley is supposed to be golfing. The course has a nice smooth paved cart path, which I will have to revisit with some friends on wheels. I skateboard around a few golf carts, scare a few geezers, and finally locate Crossley on the 8th green. He's so freaked about his buddies thinking I'm, like, a secret relative of his, that he points me over to a tree we can hide behind to talk. Like *that* doesn't look weird.

Anyway, I fake like Christina and I are new best friends and tell him she insisted I talk to him here. I want to test out his reaction to something, so I say, "I think we've found the lost dogs." (I must be psychic, because probably by that moment it was true!) The lid's pretty sealed on his emotions, too, but I see this little tightening around his lips and eyes. Is it fear? After he gets control of himself he says, in a very proper voice, "I'm sure Christina will be overjoyed if you've found Redley. We'll certainly have a reward for you."

Interesting, I think, that all he cares about is *her* dog. Could mean that he's not the one who did it after all. Or not. Maybe his real fear is that some thrasher like me could ace him out in retrieving his little darling's lost pooch. Anyway, his eyes go all wide as he sees something over my shoulder. I turn. His golf buddies are staring at us. "I'll tell Momma the payments will be on time this month," I call, and thrash on down the golf path.

RANDY'S REPORT

Darwina Lopez, DVM: I called to set up an appointment with her. She said to meet her at her clinic because she had a dog to check up on. The clinic is a pretty nice place. Lots of toys for dogs to play with and soft beds for them in the waiting room. Darwina's motorcycle was outside. She seems kind of unusual for a vet, but after talking to her I'm convinced she's really good at her job.

She's really worried about the missing dogs. A lot of her clients are from the kennel club, and she says every day she hears about another dog gone.

She's also very puzzled about the sick and starving dogs that Dooley has been bringing in to her. She was curious enough about it to do an autopsy on a few of the dogs that had died. She found fur and bones in their stomachs. It was as if the dogs had been living in the wild. In fact, not "as if." Darwina thinks that's the whole problem. These dogs have been living in the wild and doing the best they can. But they're not equipped for it. So they get sick or starve.

What she really can't figure out is why they'd be living in the woods when food is so much more easily available from inhabited areas. The other thing she can't figure out is why all the ones she's seen are purebreds. They're the ones who are most likely to be watched closely by their owner. So that's another puzzle.

I also asked her about TheDogBytes.com. She said anyone can read it, but only very special "dogs" can post. She wasn't willing to tell me any more about it, but it gave me the feeling she's in the club. I guess it makes sense they want who does it to be a secret. If people don't know, it keeps up the fiction that dogs are in charge. It makes people think harder.

When I asked about the messages telling dogs to escape to Dog Wood, she figured it was just someone using the situation to promote a certain philosophy. She didn't have much more to say about it; I think she's too busy taking care of dogs to try to figure out what's going on.

Mr. Norris: I got his address from the phone book and found him in front of his house, mowing his lawn. He remembered that Jack was my friend and asked how Mara was doing. I said good, and told him about finding Joe. He seemed happy to hear it and generally willing to help. But he didn't know what happened to the missing dogs. He had enough dogs on his hands already.

I asked him about Peter Frost and Canigen. He didn't seem to mind the questions. He said sure, sometimes Frost adopts dogs from the pound. Norris lets him. "Canigen is a legitimate operation," he said. "They're not killing dogs over there or anything. It's better than what'll happen to them in the pound, if no one takes them."

I must have made some kind of face, because suddenly his mouth drooped and his eyes got kind of hard. "Let me give you a bit of data," he said. "If every family in this town adopted dogs tomorrow, we would *still* have to put to sleep a lot of dogs by the end of the next week. That's how much oversupply there is. And it's not the dogs' fault, it's the human beings."

That left me speechless. His face looked so tired. I saw a glimpse of something—I think at one time he used to really care, but he's been so worn down by the sheer numbers that now he's just kind of given in.

Mr. Kuo: He wasn't too happy about me calling him at home on a Sunday. But once I explained some of the evidence we've been tracking, he agreed to see us tomorrow before the hearing. He's going to have the committee look into the whole problem tomorrow night at City Hall. I asked if he could get the police to help out. He said he'd look at our evidence and then decide. There will be two cops at the hearing, anyway. He doesn't want it to get out of hand again.

JACK'S REPORT

Name: Dooley / Genus: Dog Catcher / Species: *curmudgeonis*

Traits: Large neck. Watchful eyes. Unkempt coat.

Habitat: the one in which he seems most comfortable is his truck. My assistant Mara and I rang the bell of his house, but he preferred the truck environment. We heard a great deal of barking from inside the house. I asked if he had a lot of dogs. He glanced around nervously. "Shh!" he said. "They need a home. But don't let the neighbors hear." Mara and I shuddered to imagine what the inside of the abode looks like.

Uses: Really knows how to catch dogs. We watched him in action. Every dog that we saw, he was able to lure to his truck with no problem. Dogs seems to love him. This is a paradox. Is it because he understands them so well? Or is he just so sly that he's got everyone fooled?

His other talent, we discovered, is that of Webmaster. While he was out conversing with a dog, Mara suggested that his glove compartment might accidentally fall open. Documents happened to spill out containing, among other things, HTML code. A serial number on one document looked familiar. I quickly matched it to a number I had in my MicroJack database: the server number we found in the TheDogBytes clubhouse.

Field Notes: When confronted, Dooley admitted

to being the founder of TheDogBytes.com. He insisted that all he did was maintain the site, whose purpose is to let dogs have their say.

"Why be so secret about it?" I queried.

He shrugged. "Would anyone pay attention to it if they knew it was me? Besides, it's more fun that way. I let a few chosen friends help out. We want to make people think about how dogs really feel."

I then asked him who was encouraging dogs to abandon human companionship and take refuge in Dog Wood. A troubled look came into his eye. He whined a bit and said those were unauthorized messages. Someone had broken into the server and given themselves access. He tried to block them out, but they had installed ways to get around that.

Dooley had that guilty look that one recognizes so easily on a canine face. I asked him what was bothering him. He burst out with an impassioned plea for me to believe that he was not the one taking the missing dogs. Some interloper in his territory was making him look bad. In fact, he said, he was about ready to quit his job and go look for the lost dogs himself.

This sentiment seemed genuine. However, we must put our emotions aside to analyze the behavior. Where does his guilt come from? Could it be that he's not fully in control of his own actions? Perhaps he cannot resist taking dogs. Clearly he has some deep connection to them, much more so than to humans. It is possible that he steals the dogs, takes them someplace, and then regrets it very much later on—especially when he is on the verge of being caught?

Postscript: I do not mean to accuse Dooley. Only to put forward a theory. I also asked if he had lost some wirecutters. "No, I've got mine. Why?" he said.

Name: Molly and Mark / Genus: ARFerus / Species: *rabidus*

Traits: Near-feral. Disorderly hair. Natural fabrics. Moral superiority. Love all animal species, with the notable exception of Homo *sapiens.*

Habitat: This pair was found at the ARF headquarters, a storefront not too far from my own house.

Uses: Dogs' best friends. Or so they say. It is true that they have done a lot of good for dogs. They make owners think about how they treat their dogs. They provide an anti-

dote to the breeders' fixation on purity.
And they put pressure on the pound to treat
dogs well.

Field Notes: The problem is, they seem to lack
a sense of proportion. For instance, they
act like Dooley is evil incarnate. Judging
from my visit with him, that is an overre-
action. If he is the one taking the dogs,
he is sick rather than evil.

I then questioned them about Peter
Frost's accusation that they poured blood on
his car. They didn't admit to doing it, but
they did say he deserved it and besides it
wasn't really blood. I cannot judge the mer-
its of Frost or his lab. But as a scientist,
I am torn on the issue. Research must be
done to help both humans and animals. Yet
at the same time, some of the things that
are done in those labs would make your skin
crawl.

Molly stated her belief that what Frost
and the breeders are really working toward
is the day they can clone dogs for profit.
That way they can control all genetic vari-
ation. They'll be able to do away with the
real thing. The reason this is so bad is
that purebreds go against the natural evolution of the dog. She wants the species to
be able to reach its highest potential.

"It's their natural right," she said.

I opined that evolution is not concerned with natural rights: just look at all the species it's allowed to go extinct. Mark responded that now there's a new force in the equation—the human race. Our technology has given us too much power. It is our duty not to cause any more extinctions, nor to hold back other species. I replied that if he thinks our technology has given us too much power now, just wait thirty years. This seemed to fill him with uncontrollable rage. Luckily he realized I was not personally to blame and said very calmly, "That's just exactly what I mean."

I then set a trap by saying, "You use technology for TheDogBytes.com, don't you?" He hardly batted an eye. He said he was just trying to give dogs the same tools humans have.

So we have a conundrum. Dooley reluctantly admitted to starting the site. Mark and Molly seem to embrace it as theirs. Someone must be lying. Still, that would not be enough to pin the dognappings on them. The various bits of commentary found on the site may just be someone taking advantage of the situation to promote their own point of view.

When I asked them what they thought about the missing dogs, Molly said she thought Canigen Labs was the likely culprit. She offered her services in helping to catch them. Mark agreed, but he also put on a bemused smile and said, "Or who knows, maybe the dogs really are just fleeing to Dog Wood on their own."

"So maybe you were the ones with the wire-cutters at the dog show?" I said.

"Wasn't that fantastic?" Molly responded. "I'd like to shake that person's hand."

One thing I will say, they don't try to cover up their beliefs. They seem to have a strong motive for "liberating" dogs, but would they go so far as stealing them? And how would this explain the sick and hungry dogs?

You put down the last page and rub your eyes. Your head is spinning with the possibilities. You comfort yourself with the fact that at least you've discovered Dog Wood. The dogs can be rescued tomorrow, even if you still don't yet know who put them there.

11

DOG WOOD

The call comes at six in the morning. It's Randy. "Canigen Labs has been hit. Meet me in ten minutes. Bring the JackPack."

You bat your eyes open, pull on your clothes, do a few strokes with the toothbrush, grab a breakfast bar, throw on a coat, and head outside. Randy's walking across the street, rolling two bikes along with him. This confuses you, because there's another bike lying on your front lawn.

You don't quite recognize it in the gray dawn light. But you do when you get closer. It's yours. Both of the tires have been slashed. The frame is mangled. That's not what scares you, though. "They know where I live," you say slowly. "And they're sending a message."

Randy stares at the bike. "I guess so. We'll have to check it for prints. But right now, we need to get going. Someone broke into Canigen Labs last night. Twelve dogs are gone."

Your brain isn't fully operational yet, so you just get on the bike Randy has brought and start riding. But about halfway there, you begin to wonder: What if the culprit is Peter Frost?

Then again, how could it be? His lab was just hit. Unless . . . it's all a ruse.

You keep on pedaling. The fact that you're with Randy makes you feel a lot safer. You go down along Airport Road, up the drive to the business park, and join a knot of reporters, Canigen employees, and police officers outside the lab building.

Peter Frost gives you a warning look the moment he sees you. You try to approach, but he puts a quick stop to your offer of help. His genial manner is gone. "Look, you've meddled enough. The dogs have electronic tags. We'll be able to track them. Now just let everyone do their jobs."

You and Randy can only shrug and deposit yourselves on the sidewalk where you parked your bikes. "I guess it wasn't worth getting out of bed after all."

But you're staring at the trees at the edge of the parking lot, and the hill above them. "Dog Wood is right over that ridge," you say.

Randy jumps up. "Let's go!"

Soon you're on your bikes and huffing up the steep fire trail to the top of the ridge. You ride along the top, at eye level with the lowering rain clouds that will soon open up on Crescent Bay. Then you take the second turnoff, go down the hill, and cut into the hidden trail leading to Dog Wood.

You get off your bikes at the creek. The water's cold on your feet this gray morning, but you hardly notice. You ride very cautiously up toward the little camp where you first encountered the barbed wire fence.

A sigh of relief escapes when you see that no one is there. One collie comes up to the fence to inspect you, but the other dogs are either asleep or somewhere else in the wood.

"Should we rescue these dogs?" you wonder.

Randy shakes his head. "No time right now. We need to try to figure out who's keeping them here first. Besides, the dogs aren't going anywhere, with this fence."

You nod, get out the JackPack, and start to investigate.

DIGITAL DETECTIVES

It's time for your
final investigation.

http://www.ddmysteries.com

and enter the key phrase

DOGWOOD

When you've finished
the investigation,
the web site will
give you a page number
to return to.

You madly stuff your investigation tools back into the JackPack. Randy's already on his bike. "Come on! Come on!"

"We can't go back on the trail!" you say.

Randy points his bike straight down the hill. "We'll have to ride cross-country."

The voices are getting closer. You have no choice. You just try to stick right behind Randy and do everything he does. He follows the line of the fence, where at least a little bit of brush has been cleared away. Still, every two seconds you must dodge a tree branch, or a rock, or lift up on your handlebars to jump a fallen trunk. The memory of yesterday's crash is fresh in your brain. It focuses your mind wonderfully.

Randy cuts over to the right, heading back in the direction of the creek. By now he's slowing down. It seems you've eluded whoever was coming. You splash across the creek again, and then push your bikes up a steep embankment to get back to the fire trail. Randy claps you on the back. "You get the extreme riding prize for the month!"

The two of you cruise back into town. It's still early, so you stop by Jack's house and tell him about your adventure.

"Cool," he yawns, bleary-eyed. He's still in his pajamas. They're new pajamas, you observe, with dalmatians all over them. He notices you noticing. "These were the best I could do," he explains. "They don't make pajamas with pictures of mutts."

You sit in the breakfast nook of Jack's kitchen. He's the only one in his family who's up. Mara watches his every move from her spot in the kitchen. Randy is very excited about your latest investigation. "I think we might have enough evidence now to nail the dognapper," he says.

Jack nods. You know he's not going to be good for much until he has his bowl of crunchies.

"There's one more thing," you say. "We were going to ask all the suspects where they were around three yesterday afternoon. That's when I was attacked in Dog Wood."

"Right!" Randy says. "We did that last night, after we got your report."

"And?"

"Let's see—Peter Frost said he was in the lab . . ."

"Yeah, but he could have had enough time to drive over there before I got there on my bike."

"But he just had his own dogs stolen," Jack objects.

"I know," you say. "But it could be a trick to get us off the scent. He said they were electronically tagged. So he could be making a big deal about this, knowing all along that he can easily get the dogs back."

"It's possible," Randy agrees. "Anyway, Molly and Mark said they were hiking with three other friends. They gave us their numbers and said we could call them to confirm. Dooley said—well, he said he couldn't remember, but he was probably taking some dogs for a walk. Crossley said he was in the 19th hole. Houston Smith said it was none of our darn business."

"That's it?" you ask.

"They were the ones who answered their phones. But I thought we did pretty well."

✳ ✳ ✳

Pretty soon it's time for school. You're still thinking about who might be the dognapper. You talk it over with the other Digital Detectives, and do some more work in the Crime Lab after school. Before you know it, it's time to head down to City Hall.

Mr. Kuo has agreed to meet you before the hearing starts. He leads you, Tina, Jack, and Randy to the room where it will be held. You sit down with him at the head table and review all the evidence you've collected. At first he's a little impatient, but when he sees how well organized your investigation is, you can tell he's impressed.

Kuo consults his watch. "It's almost time for the hearing. Can you tell me who did it?"

You nod. But before you speak, two policemen walk in. They're your old friends, Officer Gallegos and his partner Pardelli. You're glad to see them. They were present when you solved your first case, so you know they'll listen to you.

The officers greet all of you and mention they're assigned to keep order at the hearing. Kuo tells them that you were about to name the person responsible for Crescent Bay's missing dogs.

"So who is it?" Gallegos asks. "Who should we arrest?"

You glance up. People are starting to file in. Mr. Norris. Dooley. Peter Frost. Darwina Lopez. Molly and Mark. Mr. Crossley and Christina. Houston Smith. They're all here.

You take a deep breath and prepare to announce the name.

It's time to name the culprit.
Go to:

http://www.ddmysteries.com
and enter the key phrase **CRIMELAB**

Do not read ahead!

"It's Peter Frost, of Canigen Labs," you say to Kuo. "He needs purebreds for his research."

After Mr. Kuo has explained to the assembled audience that the missing dogs have been found in "Dog Wood," he dispatches the two police officers. Gallegos and Pardelli march over to Frost. He jumps to his feet angrily. "What do you think you're doing?" he demands.

"You're under arrest for stealing dogs," Pardelli answers.

Frost's face goes red. He glares up at the front of the room, his eyes searching until he finds their target . . . you. "You're the one behind this ridiculous accusation, aren't you?!"

"It's your just desserts, son," Houston Smith says to Frost. "You helped steal my dog's DNA."

Frost shakes his fist at you. "That was confidential information! I never should have trusted you."

Now Crossley jumps up. You get his fist shaken at you, too. "I knew you were a bunch of meddling, cat-brained—"

Christina shrinks in her seat next to him. You know from Tina's report that it was Christina's fault that the information leaked out. But she doesn't dare tell her father.

"Calm down, everyone," Mr. Kuo breaks in. "Now, these detectives say they have evidence."

"Evidence," Frost scoffs. "All you need to do is look at where the dogs are being kept. Out in the woods.

Why would I keep dogs there when I have a facility of my own?"

"I wondered about that, too," you respond. "Then it hit me. You had so many dogs you ran out of room. The wood was a kind of holding pen while you decided whether they were useful for your research."

Suddenly Frost becomes very calm. "Fair enough. Look, I'm a scientist. Let's be objective about this. Let's look at the evidence. My guess is that you don't have one single set of my fingerprints on anything connected to the crime."

Frost comes to the front of the room. Jack opens up his laptop. Together, you review the evidence. As you do, a really bad feeling comes over you. Blood flushes through your body, causing your skin to tingle.

Jack confirms what your own eyes have already told you. "Uh, it looks like it's true. Mr. Frost's fingerprints don't match up with any of our key evidence."

Oops! After apologizing a great deal to Peter Frost, you reconsider your choice of culprits.

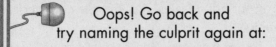

Oops! Go back and
try naming the culprit again at:

http://www.ddmysteries.com
and enter the key phrase **CRIMELAB**

"I'm sorry to say this," you tell Kuo, "but it's Dooley."

After Mr. Kuo has explained to the assembled audience that the missing dogs have been found in "Dog Wood," he sends Pardelli and Gallegos to the back of the room for Dooley.

To your surprise, Dooley does nothing to resist. He just blinks several times as the officers bring him forward. "Why would I steal dogs and put them in the woods?" he asks.

"Because you don't think owners take good enough care of them," you answer. "Plus, you're the only suspect who could not account for his whereabouts on Saturday afternoon, when I was chased through Dog Wood."

Dooley thinks for a minute. "I was on the Internet on Saturday afternoon. After Jack visited me, I was on the web site."

"That's easy enough to check out," Jack answers. He opens up his laptop and makes a wireless connection to the Web. "Can you come up here and help me check your log?"

Dooley shrugs. The officers bring him to the head table, where he helps Jack navigate to the right place. After a minute of checking the logs, Jack announces, "It's true. Dooley was on-line during the time of the attack in Dog Wood."

Dooley gives you a terribly hurt look. "I didn't do it," he says in a small voice.

"I'm sorry," is all you can say. You keep repeating it

over and over. Amazingly enough, Dooley's hurt never turns to anger. Which, in a way, makes you feel even worse.

 Try to make up for it by
naming the culprit again at:

http://www.ddmysteries.com
and enter the key phrase **CRIMELAB**

Kuo waits expectantly for you to name your suspect. You say who it is in a soft voice, so that only he and the other Digital Detectives can hear.

"Whoa, whoa, whoa," Randy objects. "I seriously doubt that's who did it."

"Are you sure?" you ask.

"Let's review the evidence again," Jack says, opening his laptop.

You look up and realize the whole room is watching. "Heh heh, sorry folks, this will just take a minute."

You go over all the clues one more time with Randy, Jack, and Tina. By the time you're done, they've convinced you that your choice can't be right.

"Sorry again, everyone," you announce to the room. "Small misfire there. We'll get this all straightened out in a minute."

With sweat starting to pour down your back, you return to the Crime Lab to figure out again who really did it.

Try again!
Go to:

http://www.ddmysteries.com
and enter the key phrase **CRIMELAB**

"It's Molly and Mark," you say, pointing them out.

After Mr. Kuo has explained to the audience that the missing dogs have been found in "Dog Wood," he dispatches Pardelli and Gallegos to arrest the culprits. They march down and converge on the ARF members. Molly sits serenely still, sure they're heading for someone else. But when Gallegos announces she and Mark are under arrest for stealing dogs, she shoots up from her chair.

"Are you crazy?" she shouts. "Why would *we* be stealing dogs? Especially purebreds?"

"You thought you were saving them," you answer. "You hate people who turn dogs into objects for sale. You hate the idea of purebreds. So those are the first dogs you wanted to 'liberate' in your campaign. You took them to Dog Wood because you had ideas about returning them to the wild. But when you found out that what the dogs really wanted to do was return to their owners, you built a fence to keep them in."

"Breeders break a dog's spirit," Molly replies. "That much is true. And so do certain other people. Like your friend Randy there, who cut off his own dog's tail."

"So *you* must be the one who sent those messages supposedly from Joe!" Randy exclaims.

Molly can't suppress a smirk. "I'll admit to that. How would you like to lose a limb? You hurt Joe. But that has nothing to do with dognapping. Where's the evidence to prove your accusation?"

Jack stands up and begins listing some of the clues you found. Fingerprints, footprints, invoices for large amounts of dog food, evidence from the camp . . .

"But the thing that convinced us," you add, "was when you claimed you were out hiking with five people on Saturday, the day I was chased in Dog Wood. The problem is, there are only two sets of bootprints on the trail to the wood. I bet they'll match up to your and Mark's boots. The prints are in a narrow line. If you went with other people, there'd be more prints, and the prints would be more spread out. You're the only ones who used that trail, to bring food to the dogs."

"So *that's* why dogs were going hungry," Darwina breaks in. "You kept them in the woods. Not all the dogs were able to get to the food you brought, so they starved. Or got sick or injured."

"They would have learned!" Molly replies heatedly. Then, realizing what she's just said, she covers her mouth.

"I'm sure when the police finish investigating the theft at my lab, they'll have yet more evidence against you," Peter Frost says.

"I suspect we'll also be able to trace the break-in at TheDogBytes.com headquarters to you," Jack mentions. "Same with the messages telling dogs to go to Dog Wood."

"That's what that web site should have been used for all along," Molly states.

Then a woman you don't recognize stands up. "She's the other ARF person I talked to," Randy whispers.

"You've done some admirable work, Molly," she says. "But you've crossed over the line with this."

"It was for their own good!" Mark declares defiantly as Pardelli and Gallegos take him and Molly by the elbow. "There's a higher law than yours!"

"Maybe," Gallegos replies as the two officers lead them from the room. "But I still suggest you find a lawyer who knows ours."

12
EVERYONE GETS A TREAT

"I'll be doggoned," Tina says with a straight face. She, Randy, and Jack are staring at an engraved card delivered by hand to your house. It's an invitation to the Highlands Kennel Club on Saturday afternoon. The members want to thank you for finding the missing dogs.

"Did all of them belong to kennel club members?" Tina wonders.

"Not all," you answer. "But more than half of them did. At least that's what Mr. Kuo said."

"I hear that Dooley did a good job of rounding them up from Dog Wood," Jack adds. "He had them all in the pound by Tuesday evening, so that the owners could come and claim them."

"And Mr. Norris told me a bunch of other people came to the pound too," Randy says. "A lot of dogs got new homes this week."

"I think I'd rather go to a party at the pound than at the kennel club," Tina remarks.

"Yeah, it's too bad the kennel club people don't use some of their money for those dogs at the pound," Randy says.

"Well, I still want to go to the club on Saturday," Jack says. "The invitation says our families are invited too. Mara's never seen a place like that. Plus, I'll bet the food will be really good."

"We should go," Randy agrees. "There may also be a reward check coming our way."

Tina's eyes brighten. "I'm there."

* * *

Saturday comes and you all get decked out in your finest garden party clothes. Your whole family goes, along with Tina and her dad, Randy, his parents, and Joe, and Jack and Mara. Christina Crossley, wearing white Capri pants and a spotless white blouse, greets you at the gate like homecoming heroes. She can't quite look you in the eye, though. You figure it's because she's still allowing her dad to think you're the ones who spilled the beans about his gene-splicing deal with Canigen.

In spite of that, Mr. Crossley is cordial to you. He introduces you to other grateful members, who are equally pleasant. You notice that the event has even gotten Crossley and Houston Smith in the club at the same time. They keep on opposite sides of the patio from one another, though.

At one end of the patio is a barbecue pit with a huge slab of meat turning on a spit. The four Digital Detectives gather around an umbrella-covered table near the pit. The smell of the meat makes your mouth water. You're not the only one. Joe and Mara have planted themselves in front of it, drool dripping off their muzzles. Amazingly enough, they are the only two dogs to do so. The rest are out on the lawn, doing tricks and generally obeying their masters.

"Mara!" Jack commands. "Move away from there. None of the other dogs are begging. You can't act like that here."

Tina snorts. "I still say there's something creepy about

how well-behaved these dogs are. Like they've bred the *dog* out of them. You know, Molly was right about some things."

"Maybe so," you agree. "But she went too far."

"There's one thing about her I didn't understand," Randy says. "Why did she hate Dooley so much? It seems like they both appreciated the same qualities in dogs."

"Well, he wouldn't let them join TheDogBytes.com," Jack answers. "I was helping him reconfigure his server the other day. It's obvious that Molly and Mark had broken into it just before we first found the clubhouse, so that they could post their messages about Dog Wood."

"And maybe there was something else, too," you muse. "They both love dogs, but they had different philosophies about them. Molly thought dogs ought to return to the wild. She didn't take into account the fact that they can't survive out there by themselves. So she didn't like it when Dooley started finding dogs who were sick and hungry."

Christina appears with a tray of lemonade. Lindsay brings along a plate of little snacks you learn are called canapés. They're a bit smelly. Jack ignores them in favor of a tray of squirrel-shaped frosted cookies.

After she's handed out the lemonades, Christina smiles her bright smile. "Are you ready?" she whispers.

Before you can ask for what, you hear a *ding ding ding*. It's her father, tapping a spoon on an empty glass. Once he gets the attention of all the members, he proposes a toast to you, the Digital Detectives. Everyone raises their glass and gives you a cheer.

But that's not all. Crossley also announces that he has a generous check for you, in recognition of your good work in finding Redley and the other members' dogs. Amidst applause, he holds the check in the air as he brings it over to you.

But Houston Smith cuts in front of him. "And," Houston bellows, "I've written you a reward check of my own. For uncovering some other nefarious doings among some of our club members."

Houston ceremoniously places the check on the table in front of you. He shakes all your hands and leaves without a glance at Crossley, who stands rigidly a few feet away. Crossley clears his throat, then comes forward, trying to pretend nothing happened.

It's a bit embarrassing. You don't know quite what to do, so you just shake his hand, take the check, and say, "Thank you very much."

Crossley makes a small bow and leaves. Tina grabs the check. "Wow," she breathes, staring at the amount. You've received rewards for other cases you solved, but this is your biggest haul yet. "What should we do with it?"

Randy gives you a little punch in the shoulder. "I know someone who needs a new bike."

"I think we should give some of it to TheDogBytes.com," Jack puts in. "Dooley spends every cent he earns on his dogs and the web site."

"Good idea," you agree.

Jack nods appreciatively and picks up another frosted squirrel cookie. As he bites into it, he says, "This is the weirdest cookie I've ever eaten."

You hadn't been watching too closely, but now you remember where you've seen the cookies before: at Connie's pet shop.

"Jack!" you exclaim. "Those are dog biscuits!"

Jack's face curdles for a moment. But he recovers quickly. He looks calmly at what remains of the squirrel and then holds it out for Mara. "What was I *thinking?*" he says to her. "It's so rude of me not to offer you some."

Mara gulps it down. Jack adjusts his glasses on the bridge of his nose and studiously avoids looking at any of you. Instead he gazes at the meat turning on the spit over the fire. "Can we slice into that yet?"

As if in answer to his plea, a man in a chef's hat comes bustling through, carrying a large platter and a giant carving knife. Soon all of you have something good to chew on.

ABOUT THE AUTHOR

Jay Montavon lives in San Francisco. He has written more than twenty books and computer games under different pen names, including a number of books in the *Choose Your Own Adventure* series. He has also written the computer games *Journey into the Brain* and *3D Castle Creator*.

Don't Miss a Single Case!
Have you solved these exciting mysteries?

DIGITAL DETECTIVES MYSTERIES®

1#: THE CASE OF THE KILLER BUGS
Insect Invaders is the most popular game in America, but certain versions contain a deadly virus that fries hard drives like bacon and eggs! Who created the virus and why? It's up to you and the Digital Dectectives to find out. To solve the case, you'll make on-line investigations of a sinister moonlit dock, a high-tech career fair, and a mysterious warehouse.

#2: WHEN NIGHTMARES COME TRUE
When a surfer disappears near one of the creepiest beachfront mansions in Crescent Bay, the Digital Dectectives stumble onto their next big mystery. The house once belonged to an eccentric inventor, Tibias Mandrake, who performed some very bizarre experiments in his laboratory. But now that the house is on the real estate maket, some people in Crescent Bay are *dying* to get their hands on it. To solve the mystery, you'll make on-line investigations of the mansion, a pitch-black cave, and Mandrake's secret lab.

Available now in bookstores!